LEGAC

CW00434265

Left a half-share in her late aunt's cottage, Staff Nurse Rosalyn Hayward's delight is short-lived when the co-owner turns out to be the arrogant Hungarian surgeon, Max Barrington. For he is the last man on earth with whom she wants to share.

LEGACY OF LOVE

BY
HAZEL FISHER

MILLS & BOON LIMITED
London · Sydney · Toronto

First published in Great Britain 1982
by Mills & Boon Limited, 15–16 Brook's Mews,
London W1A 1DR

ISBN 0 263 74026 9

Set in 10 on 11½ pt Linotron Times
03/1082

Photoset by Rowland Phototypesetting Ltd
Bury St Edmunds, Suffolk
Made and printed in Great Britain by
Richard Clay (The Chaucer Press) Ltd
Bungay, Suffolk

CHAPTER ONE

'THERE, that's Mrs Moran. Now what about Miss Hanson? Tell me about her.' Staff Nurse Jessica Bradley smiled encouragingly at newly-qualified Staff Nurse Rosalyn Hayward, who managed a wan smile in return, as she searched her memory for the details she had so carefully learned the day before, her first on Jevington Ward, Women's Surgical.

'She isn't for op. She's just for tests and observation. Query obstruction. Complaining of difficulty in swallowing, nausea.' Rosalyn ticked off each point on her fingers. It was dreadful, having to memorise patients' names and conditions like this, rather as if she was revising for an exam, but it could not be helped.

By rights she should not have been on Jevington Ward for another month. Because they were short she had been moved from Glynde, Men's Surgical. To cap it all, Sister was on sick leave and Jessica, the senior staff nurse, would be away at a funeral the next day—Mr Barrington's ward round day. Ros had spoken to all twenty-four patients and read their case-notes as a matter of course, but the new consultant general surgeon would expect her to be spot-on, to know *every* little detail about the patients on Jevington. That she was newly promoted and had just moved to that ward would be of no consequence to Mr Max Barrington. He would expect her to *know*. Excuses would be swept aside in a brusque icy-cold manner. Of that there wasn't the slightest doubt.

'Of course, Miss Hanson is due for discharge tomorrow, so he might not be interested,' Jessie went on, kindly. 'It's just as well to know, though.'

'Be prepared, as Sister Tutor used to say!' Ros quipped with a brave attempt at humour, and Jessie giggled. It was all right for Jessie, *she* wasn't due for execution tomorrow!

'I'm sure I shall forget something important tomorrow. Something *vitally* important,' Ros went on, but Jessie shook her head, decisively.

'Not you! You'll be fine—if you don't worry too much!' Jessie added, tongue in cheek.

Ros put her hands over her ears so as not to hear yet more advice. Then she set her new cap straight yet again. It was of paper, white, with a broad blue stripe indicating the status of staff nurse, and did not sit easily on her fine honey-blonde hair.

Her big pansy-blue, almost violet eyes, were sad as she picked up the next case-folder. Poor Mrs Lloyd, who did not have long to live. 'Mrs Ann Lloyd,' she began, 'Laparotomy. Found to have inoperable carcinoma. For discharge in two days if fit enough. She's *such* a dear,' Ros went on, turning to Jessie. 'Isn't there anything we can do? Perhaps Mr Barrington . . .'

'Rosalyn!' Jessie spoke firmly, then wagged her finger at her friend, the way old Sister Smith used to do. 'You get too involved. Everything that could be done for Mrs Lloyd *has* been done. Crying won't help her. You have to be a bit harder, dear. Cold and clinical, like Mr Barrington!' she went on, and Ros shuddered.

'Please! I don't want to hear another word about Mr Barrington. He sounds like a first-class ogre! How the St Ann's grapevine has come up with so much information about him, I'll never know. The man has only just arrived!' No-one could be as black as the efficient grapevine had painted Mr Barrington.

Jessie frowned. A big girl, she leant against the desk in Jevington ward office, gazing at the patients, who could be seen through the observation panel. Her shrewd grey eyes rested briefly on Ros before she turned back to the observation panel. 'He comes over as a highly-efficient, almost brilliant clinician. We all expect consultants to be a bit distant from we lesser mortals, but from what I gather, he lives in a different world altogether. In a rarified bubble, cut off from the air the rest of us breathe, if you know what I mean?'

Ros did. Consultants got to the top of the tree through expertise, sheer hard work, guts, so why shouldn't they consider themselves a cut above mere nurses? It seemed reasonable enough to her. Apparently this Mr Barrington was different—different enough to cause comment throughout the whole of St Ann's, a medium-sized general hospital in the heart of Suffolk. According to rumour he was a well-oiled machine, with a personality like the inside of a deep-freezer on its coldest setting! Physically, he was tall, dark and very handsome, with piercing black eyes, a trim, muscular body, and a slightly foreign accent.

'I expect it's because he's foreign,' Ros said, out of the blue, and Jessie looked her surprise. 'Keeping himself to himself, I mean. Perhaps he doesn't understand English ways. Probably thinks we're all mad!'

'Maybe we are, at that,' Jessie commented, wryly. 'It's a pity I have to be away tomorrow. Sister Sinnott would have taken his round—she knows Jevington well, but she's stuck at some American airport and can't get back in time. Anyway, she doesn't know the patients and you do, now.'

'Mm. I'll do my best to cope, but the round will be a nightmare from start to finish!' Ros got up to put the case-notes away. She was nearly as tall as Jessica, but slender, a deceptive slenderness, her fragile, delicate air making people wonder how she survived the rigours of nursing. They soon learned that Ros was as tough as any of the heftier nurses and was often fresher at the end of the day than those who appeared so much stronger and more fitted to the hard physical grind.

She clenched her tiny fists. For his sake, she hoped Mr Max Barrington would not comment unfavourably on her ability to cope. She just might tell him a few home truths!

'That's it, then.' Jessie yawned and stretched, then glanced at the electric clock on the wall of Sister Ray's office. 'Nurse Conrad should be back from supper, shouldn't she? I'll go when she comes. Sure you don't want a break?'

Ros shook her head, the cap leaning precariously over one ear. She simply could not spare the time for a supper-break, though a cup of tea was always welcome. 'I'll make myself a quick cuppa,' she said. 'You'll be here till I get back, won't you?'

Jessie nodded, and Ros took a peek at her patients before hurrying to the ward kitchen. Making tea for staff, other than consultants, wasn't strictly allowed but surely one cup wouldn't hurt? She would have asked if any patients wanted a cup, but it was just after their suppertime and the night staff would make them a hot drink before settling them for the night.

Humming to herself as she worked, she tried to keep her mind busy, away from the horrors of the following day. She hadn't met Mr Barrington, of course, as he had only recently arrived, but he had already created an impression on staff and patients alike. He had visited Jevington once, on an informal getting-to-know-you visit with the retiring consultant. A visit Ros fortunately missed. A new man usually took in all the information given him, made a few neutral comments, said he was sure he would enjoy the challenge of St Ann's, then departed with a brief smile. Not Mr Max Barrington. Oh, no! He put everyone's back up, according to Jessica, including the retiring consultant's, Mr Turner, an easy-to-get-along-with man if ever there was one. This wouldn't do and that wouldn't do, the nurses were, he felt, rather slack and he hoped his wards would run more smoothly in the future than they had in the past. St Ann's needed a spring-clean. Whether he meant physically or a spring-cleaning of mental attitudes, Jessica hadn't been sure.

Mr Barrington hadn't smiled once, not even when thanking the nurse who brought in coffee for the disting-uished visitors. That was something in his favour, though, Ros reasoned. He *did* say thank you, something even junior doctors were inclined to forget.

'Not brewing tea, Nurse!' a scandalised but musical voice asked, and Ros nearly dropped the teapot in her fright. Then she smiled warmly at the houseman, Dr Ahmed, a short, roly-poly young man with a brown skin and a wide smile displaying gleaming white teeth.

'Tea-making isn't allowed,' she said, firmly, but set-ting out another cup, anyway. 'There's just enough for Jessie and me, so go away!'

'Ah, please! See, I go down on my knees and beg!' As good as his word, Dr Ahmed sank to the kitchen floor and gazed up in supplication.

Ros giggled, then the laughter died on a choking sound as she saw the tall figure framed in the doorway. A tall, dark-haired man strode in, and her heart skipped a beat. It was too early for visitors and too late for consultants, but one never knew . . .

'Can . . . can I help you?' She tried to keep her voice steady, but knew her face was flushed and her cap askew yet again. Poor Dr Ahmed hastily scrambled to his feet, even his skin tinged with a noticeable red.

'Sir! Mr Barrington! We did not expect you,' Dr Ahmed finished lamely, and the stranger treated him to a glacial stare, while Ros' flush deepened.

This was Mr Barrington! The new consultant, at whose round she was supposed to appear cool, efficient, and knowledgable. Her mind went blank with shock, and she was still struggling for some suitable comment when the dark gaze of Mr Barrington swung round to her. It gave her the feeling that a prison guard in one of those old films had caught an escapee in his searchlight, Ros being the escapee. Certain death would follow, and she shook her head, trying to clear it of the fanciful notion.

'Who is in charge of this ward?' The words were coldly spoken, with only a hint of foreign accent, and Ros struggled to find words, but the effect of those black, black eyes fixed on hers was unnerving. No doubt a deliberate ploy on his part.

'Staff Nurse Bradley, sir,' she squeaked. 'Sister is on sick leave. I'll show you to the office,' she hurried on, and Mr Barrington grunted, which presumably meant he agreed.

Flustered and wishing she was anywhere but at St Ann's, Ros led the consultant to the office where, to her relief, she found Jessica chatting to an 'up' patient, Mrs Millington.

Jessie's eyes mirrored her own horror as she jumped

to her feet. 'Good evening, Mr Barrington,' she said smoothly, and Ros had to admire the older girl's coolness. Hopefully it would come with experience.

Gently, Ros shepherded Mrs Millington out, then closed the door, hovering just inside the office, since whatever the new man had to say she ought to hear.

But that did not suit Mr Barrington. He leaned back in Sister Ray's chair, and indicated that Ros could go. When, in her surprise, she didn't move, he said, coldly: 'One nurse is quite sufficient. I do not need *two* of you hovering around me! No doubt your tea—and your young man—are getting cold!'

Ros gasped, her temper rising, and Jessica shot her a warning glance. 'This is Staff Nurse Hayward, sir. She will be in charge of Jevington tomorrow. For your ward-round,' she added, in case he was in any doubt.

His lips tightened, but he made no comment, merely carrying on his conversation with Jessica as though Ros wasn't there. 'This Mrs Lloyd. She's going out soon?'

'Yes, sir,' Jessie said, primly. 'In about two days. There isn't anything that can be done . . .' Her voice trailed off as he shot her a sharp look, and Ros was glad it wasn't her!

'I was aware of that,' he commented, then got Jessica to go through all the case-notes briefly with him, before getting up. Ros shot to her feet, belatedly remembering that she ought to have offered him coffee, or some of the by now cold tea. He was taller, much taller than she had imagined. Even her five seven shrank by comparison, and she felt positively minute as he came towards her. She swallowed, wondering whether to smile. Mr Turner always smiled at staff, but this man . . .

In the event she decided against smiling, which was just as well, as the surgeon swept by her apparently without registering the fact that she was there at all.

'Phew!' Jessie dramatically wiped her brow, her smile wry. 'Good luck to you tomorrow, young Ros. You'll certainly need it!'

'It's just incredible!' Ros flared. 'How *dare* he treat me as . . . as if I wasn't of any consequence! I don't think he even noticed I held open the door for him! I was thinking I ought to offer him a cup of tea, but it's just as well I didn't. I might have put rat-poison in it!'

Jessie laughed, and even Ros saw the funny side of it, but his attitude rankled, and she resolved to make him realise that she was as efficient and capable as any staff nurse and that St Ann's was as good as his previous hospital, a world-famous London one. It was simply prejudice on his part. If he thought so little of St Ann's, why on earth couldn't he have stayed in London?

Because of her fears that something dreadful would happen at Mr Barrington's round, Ros went on duty early next morning. Day staff hours were from 7.30 to 4.30 or 12.30 to 9.30, but trained staff were not expected to arrive before eight a.m., when the night staff gave their report and left, or to stay beyond eight p.m., when at least one trained nurse would be on duty.

Ros was on Jevington soon after seven that morning, just in case. She lacked the confidence that came with experience, and did not want St Ann's to fall short of Mr Barrington's ideal. Everything, she was determined, would go like clockwork.

Night Staff Nurse Curtis raised her brow in surprise as a pale and tired-looking Ros greeted her. 'We *are* keen, aren't we! Couldn't you sleep?' she teased.

'It's Mr Barrington's round. I wanted to make an early

start—just in case,' Ros confided, and Nurse Curtis nodded.

'I've been hearing about him. Quite a stickler. I haven't met him, but Mr Arthur's secretary says he's dishy, with enormous black eyes.'

'And a black heart, I shouldn't wonder,' Ros put in, crossly, and the night nurse smiled.

'I can see he's put *your* back up. But take heart, you're one of many,' Nurse Curtis went on. 'He upset the PNO, as well.'

'Did he? How?' Ros was startled. The Principal Nursing Officer, Miss Merry, the equivalent of the old-style matron, was a dear. Of course she had her funny little ways but was remarkably even-tempered.

'I don't know,' Nurse Curtis admitted. 'It's probably just a grapevine rumour. May not have happened.'

Ros wouldn't believe that. There must be something in it. This new man was dreadful and ought to be taken in hand. A mere staff nurse wasn't the right person to do it, though, she had to admit.

Her lips quirking at the thought of herself and the dark-eyed Hungarian having a bargy, she didn't hear the registrar enter her office. Suddenly, hands gripped her thin shoulders so tightly she almost squealed. For one terrible moment she thought it was that dreadful man!

'Caught you smiling to yourself again!' a deep voice said, and her heart resumed its normal place. 'Don't you know it's one of the first signs of madness?' Everett Scott went on, teasingly.

'If you will creep up on me like that, it's no wonder!' Ros snapped, rubbing her shoulder. Everett, a tall, rawboned Northerner, didn't know his own strength. 'Please go away,' she added.

'I'm here for the round, sweetheart! Thought I'd come in early and see what needs doing.'

'You, too?' she asked, wryly.

'*Thought* you were in early,' he commented, crossing to the cabinet where patients' notes were kept.

Ros barely spared the fair-haired giant a glance as she began the day's preparations. There was one admission booked, but she was a dental case and would not concern Mr Barrington, thank goodness. There might be others. Jevington was a busy ward.

That was one of the pleasures of surgical nursing, she found. The unexpected was always happening. She had found medical nursing a little dull by comparison, but certainly on a medical ward there was a chance to get to know patients well. On surgical the turnover was too great. But it brought its own rewards and, after a brief spell in theatre, Ros had decided she would specialise in surgical nursing.

She intended making nursing her career, had always intended it should be so. Rather a plain, quiet girl, she did not attract men easily, and whilst most of her set were married, engaged or simply living together, she led an almost nun-like existence in her big, sunny bed-sitter in the trained nurses' block. That Everett Scott was on friendly terms with her meant nothing, in that way. It was simply his nature to be on good terms with all the staff.

It took a long time to get to know Ros, and she did not always make the effort to push herself forward, to *make* people notice her. Jessica Bradley was the closest she'd got to having a friend at St Ann's, and Jessica was an acquaintance rather than a friend. Now, with the death of her much-loved Aunt Gwen, Ros was quite alone in the world.

Shrugging away the morbid reflections, Ros hurriedly went around saying good-morning to her patients, then greeted each member of staff as they came on duty. This morning there was a newly-qualified state enrolled nurse, Madge Brown, plus three students, one of them a third-year and very capable. They ought to manage well enough but unfortunately the experienced SEN, Sarah Baxter, wouldn't be on duty until the afternoon shift. This was one day Ros could have done with her moral support, if nothing else.

Ward rounds on Jevington usually commenced at nine-thirty, but Everett had brought a message from the Chief that he would start at nine as he wanted to get to know the patients. It made more of a rush for the nurses, but Ros was pleased he wanted to spend more time with his patients.

It put the consultant in a better light, and Ros was almost prepared to like him when she saw his entourage approaching. The chilly, distant expression on his face was off-putting to say the least, but Ros was nothing if not a fighter. She must make the effort to get on well with the man, for Jevington ward's sake if not her own.

'Good-morning, sir,' she smiled, and deep-set dark eyes surveyed her. He returned her greeting politely, yet it was as if he spoke to her through a pane of glass. Physically he was there, but . . . She could not explain, even to herself. It was as if he had put up mental barriers between himself and the world. Or was it just between himself and Ros Hayward? she wondered, for he seemed at ease with his registrar and the houseman.

All went well at first. Mr Barrington had a list of names and asked brief questions of Everett as he went down the list before starting the round. St Ann's wasn't a teaching hospital so there were no medical students to hang on his every word. Instead, Ros found herself doing so, as if some of his expertise could rub off on her.

At not quite twenty-two, she felt very young and gauche, and longed for the air of confidence and authority exuded by most of the ward sisters she'd known. At that moment she felt very alone. Whatever went wrong, she would be blamed. And it wasn't long before that happened.

'Mrs Ingram's case-notes, please, Nurse.' The deep, slightly-accented voice broke into Ros' reverie and she hastened to obey. She put her hand into the space in the trolley where the case-notes should have been and then went cold as her fingers touched the empty pocket. Mrs Ingram's case-notes were missing!

Shock held her silent for a moment, then Mr Barrington held out his hand, impatiently.

'I . . . I'm sorry, sir,' she murmured, trying to keep the unease out of her voice. 'They aren't where they should be. It's very odd,' she went on, almost to herself, then winced as she heard the surgeon's exaggerated sigh.

'Do patients' notes disappear often, Nurse?' he asked, coolly, and she swung round to face him. The darkly handsome face and eyes were expressionless, almost as if he *expected* something to go wrong at St Ann's.

Fierce pride in her hospital flooded over Ros, and she shot him a reproachful glance. 'I haven't known it happen before, Mr Barrington,' she said, equally coolly, then, methodically, she went through every folder, searching for the missing case-notes.

Normally case-notes were kept in a big grey steel cabinet in the corner of the ward office. During a consultant's round the notes were removed and put in a trolley arranged on similar lines to the cabinet, with a concertina-type cardboard pocket for each folder. It was through this that Ros was feverishly searching. She went through every folder, thinking that the nursing notes might have somehow been caught in someone else's. All the time she could feel cold, accusing eyes on her. Mr Barrington had stopped talking. There was deadly silence in the office, and Ros' face was burning by the time she had finished her fruitless search.

Then, with a sinking feeling in her stomach, she went through the empty pockets in the cabinet. Nothing, except those case-notes belonging to the dental consultant. Excusing herself, she hurried out to find the SEN, who was going round the ward, tidying.

'Nurse Brown, someone's notes are missing!' she whispered, breathlessly. 'Have you any idea where they might be?'

'All the notes were in the trolley, Staff. I put them there myself,' Nurse Brown assured her, then her face changed. 'Oh, Staff! I forgot! That little student asked if she could read some of them. You were busy in the side ward and I told her it would be all right. But she would have replaced them,' Nurse Brown assured her, swiftly.

Ros' heart flipped. Student nurses had a habit of forgetting things like that. Junior students did not always appreciate that case-notes must be returned to the cabinet or the trolley immediately, and certainly must never leave the ward office.

'Was it Nurse Atkins?' She did not need the SEN's quick nod to know the name of the culprit. Nurse Leonora Atkins was a constant headache. She seemed to have two left hands and two left feet, and at least eight arms that were a trap for the unwary. It wasn't as if the girl was straight out of Introductory Block, either. Jevington was her second ward. She ought to know better. Ros knew she ought to send the enrolled nurse in

search of the missing student and, presumably, the
missing notes, but she simply could not go back to Mr
Barrington empty-handed.

She found Nurse Atkins in the sluice. Leonora
Atkins, a short plump girl, beamed at her, and Ros
didn't have the heart to give the girl the ticking-off she
deserved, if she *was* responsible for mis-filing Mrs Ingram's notes. The SEN ought to have known better than
to let anyone take case-notes when an important round
was imminent.

'Mrs Ingram's case-notes are missing, Nurse Atkins.
Did you replace them when you finished?'

The girl's guilty flush told Ros all she needed to know.
'Where are they?' She tried to keep her voice calm and
gentle. An abrupt, hectoring manner would simply
make matters worse.

'I . . . I forgot them! Oh, Staff, I'm ever so sorry. Miss
Taynor said if she had any more bad reports, she'd have
to deal with me!' Nurse Atkins wailed, big china-blue
eyes fixed on Ros in entreaty.

Ros gazed at her sadly. When she was unhappy or
angry the pansy-blue of her eyes deepened to a dark
violet. They became beautiful then, but she wasn't
aware of it. 'Please try to remember where you put
them. Mr Barrington is waiting for them, Nurse.' With
an effort she kept her voice steady. 'We'll have a talk
about your problems later,' she promised, and relief
shone out of the girl's eyes.

'I'll get them, Staff. Think I left them in the day-
room,' she began, then her horror-struck expression
told Ros that there was someone behind her. The uneasy, prickling sensation at the back of her neck told her
who it was.

Slowly and reluctantly she turned, to find Max Barrington brandishing a folder. He had found Mrs Ingram's case-notes.

'They *were* in the day-room, Nurse.' He addressed his remark to Leonora, who went scarlet, then began to shake.

'Oh, please, sir! I'm ever so sorry! Miss Taynor said I'd make a fatal mistake one day!' To Ros' horror, the student burst into tears, and fled, apparently to the privacy of the linen-cupboard.

Ros closed her eyes, just for a second. Retribution was sure to come swiftly and upon her own head. She waited for the axe to fall.

CHAPTER TWO

'COME along then, Staff Nurse. I haven't all day.' Mr Barrington's testy words sunk into Ros' brain, and the dreadful feeling of impending doom left her. The inquest wasn't going to be yet!

It was only a temporary reprieve, but at least they could get the ward round over with first.

'Tell me about Mrs Ingram,' he commented, when they were back in the office. The consultant's tone was cool, professional, not angry in the least, and Ros took heart from it.

She searched her memory for the details. 'She has cholecystitis, sir. It's a chronic condition which has now . . . now subsided sufficiently for surgical intervention.' Heavens, she thought, I sound like a surgical textbook! She gazed enquiringly at Mr Barrington, wondering what else he wanted to know.

He was shaking his head and for one awful moment Ros thought she had joined Mrs Ingram's name to another person's illness! 'That is not what I want! Tell me about the *person*. What kind of woman she is, her background, temperament.'

Puzzled, Ros did as she was bid. 'She's well into her fifties, sir. Has a divorced daughter living with her—plus two grand-children, who get her down. She . . . she isn't an *easy* woman to get on with, sir!' Ros' sharp eyes thought a glimmer of amusement crossed the surgeon's face, but she decided she was mistaken. He didn't have a sense of humour.

'Yes, I see,' he murmured, then got up swiftly. 'We will begin the round, Staff Nurse.'

'Yes, sir.' Relief washed over her. The sooner the round started the sooner it would finish, then she could relax a little and really get to know all she needed to about Jevington.

The small band went from bed to bed with Ros walking a step behind the consultant. Student Nurse Conrad brought up the rear, with the precious trolley containing the case-notes and the Kardex system. The round took longer than Ros feared for Mr Barrington spent more time with each patient than she had ever known a consultant take, and it was evident that the ladies appreciated it.

With his patients he was a different man. Certainly not jovial or even very friendly, but somehow he seemed human. Compassion exuded from his manner and the patients were quick to pick it up. Suffering and pain gave people a heightened awareness, Ros found. They knew when someone cared. They knew when a nurse or doctor was merely heaping meaningless platitudes on them, when they really wanted to know the truth or as much of it as their individual personalities would allow them to accept.

He paused longest at Mrs Lloyd's bed, and Ros' eyes darkened with a mental pain she must keep to herself. Poor woman. Only fifty, with an ailing husband, plus a small business to run. Time was running out for her.

At last they moved towards the office, and Ros let out a scarcely audible sigh of relief. It was over! Then the surgeon's dark eyes met hers and it was as if she'd been plunged into a bucket of icy water. Of course! She had almost forgotten the contretemps over Mrs Ingram's case-notes. Mentally, she braced herself for the surgeon's anger, after she had sent Nurse Conrad to make the coffee. She didn't dare entrust even that simple task to Nurse Atkins at present. It might mean another black mark for Staff Nurse Hayward!

Then, relenting, she called Nurse Conrad back and asked her to see that Nurse Atkins made the coffee. It wasn't fair on the young student and would do nothing to boost her self-confidence to know that Staff Nurse did not even trust her with that small task.

'Which one is Nurse Atkins?' Max Barrington asked as Ros closed the office door.

'She's a student, sir,' she said, non-commitally, but seeing he expected more she had to admit that Nurse Atkins was the plump girl who had burst into tears in front of him.

He raised a brow. 'I hope she doesn't cry into my coffee,' he said, dryly, and Ros was so surprised she forgot to laugh. Another black mark for her.

Everett Scott didn't make that mistake. His chuckle sounded genuinely amused, but only Ros saw the muscle twitch at the corner of their senior's mouth. He was angry. It must be with her, and her eyes rested on him in unconscious entreaty as she apologised for Mrs Ingram's case-notes not being readily available.

He shrugged. 'Please see that it doesn't happen again, Nurse. Perhaps it was not quite fair to you to heap so much responsibility upon one so young,' he went on, and Ros opened her mouth to protest. 'How old are you?' he asked, more gently.

'Nearly twenty-two, Mr Barrington,' she replied, primly.

'Ah! A great age,' he said, solemnly, and this time she *did* see a glint of humour there. The wretched man was laughing at her!

He was about to say more when the telephone shrilled. Quick as a flash he picked up the receiver, and listened intently.

Surely not an emergency? Ros' mind ran over the ward situation. They were by no means full. Even if they were, the four-bedded side ward was empty. They . . .

'It is for you, Staff Nurse. Perhaps you will see that your young men do not ring you on the ward!' he went on, holding the receiver just out of her reach. 'This telephone is for ward use only.'

'I haven't . . .' she began, but, deliberately he turned to Everett and began discussing a patient.

Fuming at the unjustness of it all, Ros spoke curtly into the telephone. Whoever it was deserved a good ticking-off. A strange voice informed her that he was Mr Simpkin, Miss Gwen Liston's solicitor.

'Oh, yes. Can I help you?' Ros kept her voice down so as not to annoy the consultant still more.

'It's about the legacy, Miss Hayward. I must discuss it with you as soon as possible. Certainly this week,' the voice continued, and Ros gasped in surprise.

'Legacy? What legacy? Do you mean I've been left something?' But it couldn't be. Poor Aunt Gwen had nothing to leave except her cottage the other side of Bury St Edmunds. Surely . . . Her heart skipped a beat and she was barely aware of the solicitor's words.

Endeavouring to keep the conversation brief and trying to take in what was being said resulted in Ros hearing very little beyond the word Fairhaven. That was Aunt Gwen's cottage and she must have left it to her!

She arranged to be at the solicitor's office the following morning, and put the phone down with a sense of disbelief. She was going to live at Fairhaven. Somehow she brought herself back to earth, back to the consultant's disapproving stare as he left a few final instructions. Behind his back the registrar winked at Ros but she was scarcely aware.

Aunt Gwen had been the nearest to a family Ros had ever known, having spent the first few years of her life in a children's home. And Fairhaven was a *real* home, a place where a family might live, not just a Home with a capital H. It had been so long . . .

With a start, she came down to earth. Memories and dreams were for off-duty. Right now she had a ward to run. Then the coffee arrived. And now there was only Ros to drink it. Hopefully Mr Scott would be back, as he had to write up the consultant's instructions.

Ros saw that the subdued Nurse Atkins had forgotten the sugar but it didn't matter. She meant well. 'It looks as though they've run off and left me, Nurse,' she said, with an attempt at lightness. 'Just put it down on the corner of the desk. Mr Scott might be back.' She smiled at Leonora Atkins, whose own smile broke through like the sun after a cloudy day. The tray wobbled precariously and Ros reached out for it in alarm, but too late. Cold milk and hot water went everywhere, and Ros watched the liquid run slowly down the side of Sister Ray's desk.

A muffled sob came from the student, and Ros hastily sent her for a cloth, plus a domestic to help clear up. Thank goodness she wasn't a ward sister! Sister Ray would be back in a few days and those few days couldn't pass soon enough. Hopefully Nurse Atkins would leave Ros enough ward to hand over!

That night she thought of the dark-eyed Max Barrington constantly. Not that she dreamed of him. Indeed, she had so little sleep that she had no recollection of dreaming at all. A sleep so fitful could not contain much in the way of dreams. She kept getting up to glance at the clock. First it was midnight. Next time she woke it was nearly one o'clock. Each time the dark face of the consultant flickered before her then vanished, rather like the Cheshire cat. Only Mr Barrington, of course, wasn't smiling. Far from it. He was frowning. His brows met in the middle, she fancied, and his whole face was one big frown. No body, just a face.

Restlessly, she thumped her pillow, turned it so that she had a cool side to lie on, then tried once more to sleep. Thank goodness tomorrow she was on late. Jessie was on at eight a.m. and Ros had left copious notes for her concerning the round and the ward goings-on. The only thing she hadn't mentioned was the trouble over Nurse Atkins. That would keep. Jessie knew the girl was careless and was always ticking her off.

Poor Leonora Atkins. Ros sat up, aware that sleep was as far from her as ever. She shook her head, trying to clear it. Had she been as thoughtless as Leonora when she was a student? She didn't think so, then a half-buried memory eased itself out of the recesses of her mind. A mental picture of first-year student nurse Hayward giving her first injection. The scream that woman let out! It wasn't thoughtlessness or any lack in Ros' injection technique. After all, there was always a first time. No, it was Ros telling the patient over and over again that the injection was for her own good! Her generous mouth curved into a smile. If she was a patient and a young nurse said that to her, she would leap out of bed and inject the nurse instead!

Still smiling she drifted off to sleep and did not waken until nearly five, hot and perspiring.

It was late July. It hadn't been a particularly good summer but a mini-heatwave had arrived and looked set for a few more days. She yearned for a long, cool swim, but the beaches were miles away and she did not, as yet, have a car. Then she remembered Aunt Gwen and the legacy. Tears sprang to her eyes. Aunt Gwen had enjoyed a swim, too. Or sometimes she would perch on the edge of the pool . . . The pool! Aunt Gwen had a swimming pool at Fairhaven! But, no. The pool would be drained and cleaned out. Had been for some months, for Aunt Gwen hadn't been well since last Christmas and had spent the last few weeks at a Catholic Home being devotedly nursed by the nuns. It was her own wish. At first Ros had commuted, but the journey was too much, particularly when she was on early shift or night duty. Public transport was virtually non-existent in the outlying areas, and she'd had to rely on lifts. Then she had suggested temporarily giving up her training so that she could nurse her aunt properly. The stormy scenes there had been over that suggestion! Now she felt guilty for not insisting on nursing Aunt Gwen, but the old lady had been well cared for by the nuns.

No, she could not swim at Fairhaven. Not yet, anyway. And how on earth could she keep a place that size going? She couldn't live there *and* work at St Ann's. So many problems, but somehow she would work out a solution.

The solicitor's appointment wasn't until ten-thirty so Ros spent part of the morning browsing around the park and the shops. Because it was so hot she wore only a white halter-neck top and jeans, and looked nearer fifteen than nearly twenty-two. Her birthday was September 9th—the first birthday she would be completely on her own. No Aunt Gwen to bake a pink-iced cake, no small but useful presents hidden in odd corners at Fairhaven—behind a cushion, on the mantelpiece, inside her bed . . . Aunt Gwen had enjoyed giving people surprises. Tears sprang to her eyes and she was glad of the dark glasses. No-one must ever know how much she missed her only real friend. Oh, Aunt Gwen! she cried, inwardly, then in her agitation she didn't look where she was going, and bumped into a passer-by, a man.

'I'm sorry,' she blurted out, then her mouth opened again and stayed open. It was Mr Barrington.

'It was my fault,' he said, brusquely. 'Come along, pet.'

Astonished, Ros almost obeyed him, then realised his words were meant for the small, dainty child beside him. The little girl gave Ros a shy smile as she hurried by, leaving Ros to stare after them, perplexed.

Mr Barrington had a daughter! Perhaps more than one. She gazed around, expecting to find a wife in tow but there seemed to be just the two of them. He was married, then. There had been no word of a marriage on the grapevine, but no doubt all would be revealed in a few weeks. He was the sort who would keep his private life very private. Wistfully, Ros gazed after them until the tall figure was lost from sight. How nice to be part of a family . . . Pulling herself together, she finished her shopping then headed for Mr Simpkin's office.

She found it eventually, in some bank chambers. The name-plate was so small she would have missed it if she hadn't looked carefully. Mr Simpkin wasn't the balding old fuddy-duddy she expected. He was fairish and somewhere around forty, she judged. His pleasant smile soon put her at her ease, then he rustled a few papers about on his desk, before gazing at her with rather sad grey eyes.

'I knew Miss Liston well. She and my father were old friends. I'm very sorry about her . . . sudden going.' A faint flush tinged his plump cheeks as though he was embarrassed at almost mentioning death.

Ros smiled to put him at his ease. 'I appreciate your kind words. Thank you. But Aunt Gwen was . . . was in pain,' she faltered, 'and she's at rest now.' She couldn't speak any more and wished politeness hadn't forced her to remove her sun-glasses. She could do with them to hide behind.

'Well, to business,' Mr Simpkin said, pedantically. 'There is the question of Fairhaven, you see.'

She nodded, struggling for control. 'Yes, you were saying something on the telephone but I wasn't really listening,' she said, honestly.

'Indeed?' The solicitor looked affronted and Ros hastened to explain about the consultant doing a ward-round.

'I'm sorry if my call got you into the old gentleman's bad books,' Mr Simpkin said, formally, and Ros' lips quivered. No way was Mr Barrington an old gentleman!

'Yes, Fairhaven. It has been left partly to you. Your Aunt, I believe, felt you would not be able to cope with the upkeep on your own. For that reason she left half the cottage to the son of some old friends. No doubt she assumed you and he would share the expenses.' Mr Simpkin peered at her while she tried to assimilate the information.

Fairhaven was not to be hers! 'I . . . I, that is, I've always looked upon Fairhaven as my home,' she said, simply, and the solicitor nodded.

'I do understand, Miss Hayward. But it *is* rather a white elephant, you know,' Earnest eyes gazed into hers, and she was grateful for his empathy. Grateful, too, for the way he was putting the problem into perspective.

She knew she could not afford to run Fairhaven. Certainly she could not live there whilst she was on duty. It would have to be kept for days off and high-days and holidays. Then the squatters might move in—if they hadn't already!

'Squatters!' she said, suddenly, and the solicitor sat back.

'Squatters? At Fairhaven, do you mean?'

She nodded. 'Do you suppose there might be? I know Aunt Gwen's handyman calls there once a week to do the lawns and so on, but does he go inside?'

'I don't know. Shouldn't think so. All her furniture was put in store, you know. So the house is empty, but the handyman does have a key.'

'I expect squatters bring their own sleeping-bags or straw or whatever. No, we ought to look. Couldn't we, Mr Simpkin?' Pansy-blue eyes gazed at him, *willing* him to help.

He looked nonplussed. 'The other owner . . .' he began.

'Oh! I'd forgotten him! Who is he? If I'm sharing with him I ought to know his name!' Stupid of her to forget her co-owner. If he was old enough to worry about such things, he would soon take care of the problems.

'A Mr Max Barrington,' Mr Simpkin intoned, and Ros asked him to repeat the name. He did so, slowly and distinctly, and her world crashed about her ears. 'He's a Hungarian gentleman. His family came over when he was a child,' he added.

Her consultant was going to be co-owner! *She* was sharing her home with Mr Barrington! She groped for words, but none came. What could she say? There was no way she could tell the solicitor that Mr Max Barrington was the last person she would share with! And Mr

Barrington wouldn't be too pleased, either. That thought gave Ros some satisfaction. She was going to be unhappy with the arrangement but so was the boss. Not to mention Mrs Barrington!

For some reason she could not fathom, the idea of sharing Fairhaven with the chief's wife was much, much more unpleasant. Quite untenable, in fact.

Absently she ran her fingers through her long, honey hair, leaving it in gorgeous disarray. The solicitor's eyes followed every movement, and she began to feel uncomfortable as well as unhappy.

'When does this Mr Barrington expect to visit the cottage?' Carefully, she kept her voice neutral.

'He is on his way there now, Miss Hayward. I did suggest he might wait for you but he said he was in rather a hurry. You have a car, I suppose?' Mr Simpkin went on, expectantly, and she shook her head.

'No. There's no way I can get out to Fairhaven today, anyway. I'm on duty at twelve-thirty. I could phone and say I'll be half an hour late, but no more than that.' Even half an hour would mean poor Jessie having to go to second lunch and she would hate that. 'Perhaps on Friday I could get a taxi there. I'm off Friday and most of Saturday.' That would be better. She was in no hurry to meet up with Mr Barrington!

But Mr Simpkin shook his head, clearly disapproving. 'No, that will *not* do, Miss Hayward. It is essential that the owners meet and discuss this matter fully. I am anxious to wind up the estate,' he added, making her feel guilty for holding him up.

'All right, I'll go now. Could you get me a taxi, please?' Ros jumped to her feet. Best get the ordeal over with.

'I'll do better. I shall take you there myself.'

Ros began to protest, more because she didn't think the solicitor would drive fast enough to get her there and back in the time, but he brushed her words aside. After a quick conversation with his secretary, Mr Simpkin led Ros out to the small courtyard at the side of the building. Expecting to see an old Escort, she was astonished to see a racy sports car in emerald-green!

He chuckled, some of the lines of fatigue leaving his face. 'Always fools people. I suppose I must be a young lad at heart!'

With due ceremony he settled her into the passenger-seat and, once out of the town, the car leapt forward, simply eating up the miles.

Ros was delighted to feel the wind in her hair. Some of the tenseness left her as she rehearsed what she must say to Mr Barrington. It was all quite straightforward. There was nothing to worry about. He could not possibly blame her for this predicament. Couldn't he? a little voice mocked, but she shut it out and concentrated on the scenery.

It was a land of green fields and hedges, of flat lands. They passed through a couple of small but pretty villages but Ros barely had time to admire the roses before they had flashed past and out to the open road.

'Fairhaven next stop!' Mr Simpkin laughed, and Ros glanced at him, shyly, really seeing him for the first time. Before he had been a shadowy figure, merely the bringer of good and then evil tidings. Now she saw him as a person, and gave him a warm smile.

Something, some awareness flickered in his pale eyes, but before Ros could mentally withdraw, they were at the cottage.

Fairhaven was large as country cottages went but was far from being a mansion. It was brick-built, with creepers around the door and ground-floor windows. Ros saw that the roses were in full bloom and her heart swelled with pride. Aunt Gwen loved her roses. *Had* loved them, she corrected herself, bitterly. Now Fairhaven was hers, and whatever alterations the dynamic Mr Barrington wanted to make, she wouldn't let him. The cottage should remain as it was apart from essential repairs. It was Aunt Gwen's home. Now it was hers, a memorial to a fine woman.

Even without the furniture, each room held memories for Ros and she could not wait to roam around them at her leisure, perhaps on her day off.

Then she saw the elegant Jaguar parked by the side of the door, and her face fell. For a second she had forgotten, but it was too late to back out.

The front door was open and Mr Simpkin called up the stairs, but one person had noticed their arrival. The small girl she'd seen with Mr Barrington came leaping down the stairs two at a time.

'Hallo, Mr Simpkin! Papa said to come up.' She paused, blue eyes fixed uncertainly on Ros, then the girl smiled—a smile that plucked at Ros' heartstrings. Whatever she thought of Mr Barrington, his daughter was a poppet.

The girl held out a hand formally. 'My name is Anne-Marie Barrington. How do you do?'

'How do you do?' Ros murmured, touched by the child's old-world politeness. Something not too often seen these days! 'I am Rosalyn Hayward. I . . .'

Then a movement at the top of the stairs caught her eye and she glanced up, half-defiantly, expecting the tall, dark-eyed consultant to come running downstairs to tear her off a strip.

But a petite, strikingly beautiful blonde came instead,

and Ros looked from her to the child and back again. The resemblance was too obvious to be missed. Both had almost white hair and blue eyes.

Then Anne-Marie went to the woman and put her hand in hers, tugging at it. 'I must introduce Miss Hayward to you,' she piped up, and Ros waited, her heart like lead, for her introduction to Max Barrington's wife.

CHAPTER THREE

BEFORE the introductions could be made a familiar voice broke in: 'Is *this* the young woman, Mr Simpkin?'

Ros flinched, her eyes unwillingly fixed on the surgeon, who appeared from the sitting-room.

'Yes, this is Miss Hayward—Miss Liston's niece.' Mr Simpkin beamed at them both as Ros nervously held out her hand. It was held very briefly, then dropped, and Ros coloured fiercely. He couldn't even bear to shake hands with her!

'I expected a rather older lady,' Mr Barrington said, slowly, frowning a little as if he felt he ought to know her but did not.

He hadn't recognised her! Elation swept through her and she gave him a sunny smile—a smile which lifted her rather ordinary face and made it almost pretty. So long as he did not connect her with the young staff nurse on Jevington she would be all right. True, he might be put out because she wasn't the mature career-woman he had evidently expected, but his dislike could be no more than that.

Ros became aware that the chic Mrs Barrington was still waiting to be introduced, and she murmured, 'How do you do?' in her direction. The woman smiled, graciously, rather like royalty, Ros thought. At least one of the family didn't dislike her on sight!

Little Anne-Marie ran to her father and begged to be picked up, but his eyes were still on Ros, who moved, uneasily. She felt Mrs Barrington's eyes on her, too, and longed to escape. 'I think . . .' she began, intending to say that she and the Barringtons would have to have their discussion at a later date. Certainly there wasn't time now, and she glanced at her watch. She hadn't phoned so Jessie would expect her sharp at twelve-thirty.

'We have urgent matters to discuss, Miss Hayward.' Mr Barrington's voice broke into her troubled thoughts and, taking her firmly by the arm, he led her through the long hallway into the kitchen. In this oh-so-familiar room Ros should have been able to relax. The cooker was still there and she ran a finger over the enamel. Memories flooded back, of the teenage Ros laboriously making jam under Aunt Gwen's tuition, of the sponges that always went sad in the middle or had one side higher than the other, of a thousand and one meals Aunt Gwen had cooked for her over the years.

Oh, Aunt Gwen! Being given Fairhaven was a mistake. She ought not to have come! At St Ann's she could forget the past, immerse herself in work. In caring for others, she could forget her own heartache, the sheer, *painful* loneliness. But here that wasn't possible. She turned anguished eyes on her companion but he did not appear to notice anything amiss.

'This . . . this legacy, Miss Hayward,' he said, carefully. 'It is out of the blue. I did not expect . . .' His voice trailed off and she realised for the first time that he, too, was unhappy about the joint legacy.

'I didn't expect to be left Fairhaven, sir,' she said, unconsciously reverting to their nurse-doctor relationship, and he frowned.

'I am not so old you have to address me as "sir",' he said, curtly, and she flushed. In the wrong again.

'Do you intend to live here?' she burst out, hardly breathing until she heard his emphatic 'No!'

'Certainly I cannot live here. You will wish to do so, naturally,' he went on.

'I can't! I . . . I work in Newmarket,' she lied. 'It's too far to commute.'

He shrugged. 'If neither of us wishes to live here, that solves the problem. Fairhaven must be sold.'

'No!' she cried, grabbing his arm and shaking him a little. 'It was my home! Can't you see that? Can't you understand? I love Fairhaven!' The tears she had been denying since her interview with the solicitor welled up, and she turned away, gazing out of the window so that her weeping should not embarrass him. Oh, Mr Barrington! she cried, silently. If only I could make you understand how I feel. But he was a cold clinician, utterly without feeling except where his patients were concerned. If she was a surgical patient he might tell her he understood, that he would do his best, tell her not to worry. But as it was . . .

Strong hands gripped her upper arms and squeezed, very gently. 'I understand that you do not wish to sell your home,' he said, softly. So softly that the words only just carried to her. 'I, too, had to leave my home,' he added.

The surgeon released her immediately, but she could feel his arms still, the controlled tenderness she had barely glimpsed. Her legs felt suddenly weak, but there was nowhere to sit.

To cover her confusion she began to speak of the past glories of Fairhaven, of the dinner-parties her aunt gave, of the yearly garden-party in aid of the local Friends of the Hospital, of the regular visits to the Children's Home where Ros had spent part of her childhood because Miss

Liston was not then in a position to have her. She did not, of course, mention that she had lived in the Home. He simply would not be interested.

There was silence when she finished, but it was a pleasant, understanding silence, and she no longer felt alone and unwanted. Mr Barrington understood and the thought comforted her.

He sighed, bringing her back to earth with a bump. 'It's time to move on, I think. I have a full afternoon.'

'Yes,' she began, then stopped. She could not offer her sympathy over the extra-long list she knew he had. She must pretend ignorance, and hope he did not associate the tall, blonde Miss Hayward with the very young staff nurse he appeared to dislike so much!

'We will speak of this later,' he promised, and for one horrifying moment she thought he was going to ask for her address, but he did not. 'Mr Simpkin can get in touch with you?' he asked, and she nodded, adding:

'He's rather a dear. So kind. And that lovely car! Oh, but you haven't seen it, have you?' Uncaring that he was a senior consultant, she urged him around the side of the cottage so that he could see Mr Simpkin's sports car.

'Very racy. Hardly the type of car I would have expected,' he said, smiling a little, and Ros giggled.

'No, I expect he thinks he's the bees knees in that!'

Mr Barrington gazed at her, perplexed. 'Bees knees?'

'Oh, I forgot you're Hungarian! It's an expression . . .' She broke off as he peered at her, intently.

She wasn't wearing her sun-glasses, and pansy-blue eyes met black ones unflinchingly. All the while her instinct was to run and break all records doing so, but she was held immobile.

'Bees legs,' he said, to her relief. 'I must remember that.'

'No, it's knees!' Ros called after him as he strode away, back to his family, but he didn't seem to hear. Instead her eyes met the astonished gaze of Mr Simpkin.

Without another word she hurried out to stand by the solicitor's car, hoping he hadn't understood.

Ros did not meet up with Max Barrington again until Thursday. Jessie had just gone for her supper and Ros was talking to Muriel Moran. Mrs Moran, a tall, grey-haired lady, was for operation the next day. Ros knew how worried the patient was and did her best to reassure her.

It was a serious operation, to remove a malignant tumour. Mrs Moran was in a sorry state when admitted and very much run down. Ros knew from Jessie and Dr Scott that Mr Barrington hadn't been keen to operate then, yet delay in building up the patient might well have been fatal, too. Now Mrs Moran was a little less poorly, but that was all that could be said for her. Ros hoped that, unlike Mrs Lloyd, surgical intervention would not come too late.

Of course she had absolute faith in Mr Barrington's restorative powers. Whatever she might think of him as a person, she admired him as a surgeon and had no hesitation in telling Mrs Moran so. Even if she hadn't thought much of his abilities she would still have praised him to high heaven knowing it would give the patient confidence.

'Is he really Hungarian, Staff Nurse?' Mrs Moran asked, quietly, lying back against her pillows.

'Makes a nice change from Englishmen!' Ros quipped, letting Mrs Moran grip her cool hand. 'Rather dashing having a Magyar bending over you! You are in my power, pretty one, he'll say!' Ros went on, and Mrs

LEGACY OF LOVE   39

Moran laughed. True, it was a weak laugh but it was better than nothing.

Then the woman's pale eyes widened in surprise, and Ros sprang up from the chair. Mr Barrington was almost breathing down her neck and she hadn't heard him arrive!

'I . . . Oh, Mr Barrington!' she began, not knowing what to say.

'We were just talking about you, Mr Barrington,' Mrs Moran put in and the dark, flinty face relaxed a little.

'Indeed? I hope it was something pleasant. How are you feeling?' he asked, ignoring Ros, who stood in the approved manner, hands behind back, feet together, eyes alert. For all the notice he took she might as well have turned cartwheels down the ward.

After his brief examination, at which he *did* allow Ros to assist, he imperiously beckoned her to follow him. With a warm smile for her patient, she did so, her long legs keeping pace with him easily. He had some last-minute instructions about Muriel Moran, obviously. Or would he connect her with the Fairhaven Miss Hayward? she wondered.

Once alone in the office, the consultant turned on her, coldly furious. 'I was just in time to hear you refer to me as a "dashing Magyar"!' he thundered. 'You are in my power, pretty one!' he mimicked, and Ros went scarlet.

'Oh, please! It wasn't like that!' she began, but the surgeon wouldn't let her continue.

With a dismissive gesture, he went on: 'I will not have my parentage and nationality made the basis for ribald comments, Staff Nurse! I am a surgeon, no more and no less, whatever my nationality. Perhaps Mrs Moran will now expect me to turn up tomorrow dressed as a Hungarian gipsy, doing funny little dances all over theatre!'

The idea of Mr Barrington dashing around theatre in his gipsy boots struck Ros on the funny-bone, and she laughed. An unforgivable sin, she well knew, but it was funny!

'I . . .' she began, trying desperately to turn the laugh into a cough but not succeeding. 'I'm very, very sorry, but . . .'

'But, but! Is that all you can say! My ward is in the charge of a giggling juvenile!' he stormed, black eyes hurling thunder-bolts at her, and she flinched.

She managed to stand her ground, though afterwards she was to marvel at her own cheek. 'I've said I'm sorry I laughed, but a sense of humour is important in a nurse, sir!' she insisted. Seeing his look of amazement, she pressed home her advantage: 'We were not making fun of you, sir. I was extolling your virtues, if you must know!' she finished, hotly. Her fists were tightly clenched, but she wanted to shake the man, *make* him understand.

'My virtues?' he said, softly. 'And what virtues do I have?'

Taken aback, she fumbled for words. 'Well . . . I meant your surgical expertise, sir. You *are* a good surgeon and I said so,' she went on, more firmly, since he appeared not to be so angry.

'Aha! Your confidence in my abilities is very satisfying. Thank you.' He made a mocking half-bow, and Ros blushed again. The sarcastic so-and-so! He was enjoying her discomfiture.

'This does not solve the problem, however.' And while Ros was wondering what problem needed solving, he carried on, smoothly: 'Nothing alters the fact that several very ill patients are in your charge—and I consider you too young for that responsibility. Please,' he went on, as Ros opened her mouth to tell him that Jessie was in charge. Feeling mutinous she closed it again, and waited for the axe to fall.

'It is not fair to the patients but, equally, it is not fair to you. So much responsibility, so much worry, for such a young girl.'

It was a struggle to keep her voice down, her manner courteous, but somehow she achieved it. 'I'm not *such* a young girl, sir! I shall be twenty-two in September. In two years' time I can apply for a sister's post,' she added, her voice shaking with emotion.

There was a painful lump in her throat, a lump caused by this hateful man's lack of understanding, lack of humanity. That was it. Mr Barrington wasn't human. He was a well-oiled, well-programmed computer. He possessed no feelings, no emotions of any kind. Perhaps it was that very failing which made him the excellent surgeon people assured her he was.

She swallowed, trying to pluck up courage to tell him, but his eyes were on her, a little puzzled. Oh, no. That was all she needed! She saw his eyes on her name-badge with the name 'HAYWARD' there for all to see.

Suddenly, he wheeled around then left, closing the office door quietly behind him, and Ros let out her pent-up breath. For one awful moment she thought he recognised the name, but she was aware of the difference a nurse's uniform could make. Hayward was a common enough name, anyway.

At Fairhaven she'd worn her long, fine hair loose, but at St Ann's she swept it back into a severe bun, to make herself look older as well as to keep it out of the way. The dull uniform of white dress and navy belt was a lot different from the halter-top and jeans she'd worn before.

No, he must be memorising her name so that he could report her to the PNO! For a few seconds she felt physically sick, angry with herself for letting her temper get the better of her. Well, worrying about it wouldn't help. With a philosophical shrug, she went back to Mrs Moran. The welfare of the patients was more important than some trifling argument among staff. If she was to be dismissed, the summons to Miss Merry would come, sooner or later.

At eight p.m. she was free, with all of Friday and most of Saturday stretching before her. By rights she should have all Saturday free, but the SEN was doing a split duty and Ros had to cover for her from lunchtime until five o'clock. There would still be ample time to spend at Fairhaven, though. She could stand there, dreaming of the past, remembering . . .

Yet on Friday morning, as she stood in Fairhaven's kitchen it was not of the distant past she thought but of the present and the recent past, of Mr Barrington's compassion, of the feel of his strong, comforting arms about her . . .

She hugged herself, trying to recapture some of the magic of those few seconds. He had smiled at her, hadn't turned from her in contemptuous anger as he'd done on the ward last evening.

He must have a split personality, for there was no doubt he was two different men. Both autocratic and proud, of course, but off-duty he appeared human, more approachable.

Would he and his wife live here? He'd said not, but if the beautiful Mrs Barrington insisted, she supposed he would give in. The little girl was rather sweet, Ros mused, a sad smile flittering across her wide, pleasant mouth. A beautiful wife, a lovely daughter, an absorbing, well-paid career—what more could Mr Max Barrington possibly need?

If only he liked me a little, just the tiniest bit, she mused. But which Mr Barrington, the mean, moody consultant or the gentler one? She didn't know. Irritably, she swept her hair off her neck and secured it with a rubber-band. Despite the heat, there was work to be done at Fairhaven and she'd come prepared.

By lunchtime Ros had finished washing all the floors, rubbed the paintwork down, cleaned the cooker as best she could with water which by then was luke-warm. She'd solved the problem of water, for the handyman's home was only ten minutes' walk down the twisty lane. It meant a lot of trudging back and forth but Ros didn't mind. It was a labour of love. She wanted Aunt Gwen to know she was looking after Fairhaven, caring for it as her aunt would have wished.

Once the main services were reconnected, and the carpets laid, the furniture could be moved out of store. Ros had that in mind for the following week. Later, on her two weeks holiday, she could get everything into apple-pie order. Fairhaven would be a home once again.

Ros wiped a cobweb from her face, not caring that her face was probably grimy. She would have a bath in the Nurses' Home where there was always constant hot water. A long, sandalwood scented bath, and her hair washed. Luxury!

Washing her hands carefully, she opened her pack of sandwiches which she'd bought in the town before getting a taxi to Fairhaven. Her travelling expenses were mounting up even before she'd paid whatever was owing to the furniture repository.

The thought sobered her. This was just a dream. No

way could she live here. Oh, it was just impossible! She turned her small face upwards, as if hoping her aunt might appear in her angel-garb, wings fluttering gently while she sorted out Ros' problems.

Foolish, fanciful child! The words she'd heard so often as a child in the Home came back to her, and she repeated them aloud. No visitation from heaven was going to solve *her* problems!

'Are you?' a soft, accented voice spoke in her ear, and Ros jumped up from the cushion, her heart in her mouth. One of the objects of her thoughts stood there— Max Barrington, casually dressed in white shirt and dark slacks. A quizzical smile played around the corners of his sensuous mouth as she continued to stare.

His mouth fascinated her and she forgot to be afraid. Forgot, too, that this was the ruthless Mr Barrington, surgeon. Why hadn't she noticed his mouth before? His lower lip was full and passionate-looking. Foolish, fanciful girl, her brain told her, and she nodded in agreement with the silent voice.

'I am. Foolish and fanciful, I mean,' she said, aloud, her pansy eyes darkening as the surgeon moved purposefully in her direction.

'You . . . you and I must have a discussion, Mr Barrington,' she said, throatily, frightened at the intensity of his gaze. Did he intend punishing her physically?

Her throat felt paralysed, but she got out the words she'd been searching for: 'Your w-wife, Mrs Barrington, does she want to live here? I've cleaned up a bit, but the carpets will need shampooing when they come back,' she rushed on, telling him of items that needed washing, or replacing.

He heard her out in silence but he was so close, so

near. *Too* near! She could have put out a hand and
touched him. Indeed she longed to do so.

'About what are you feeling foolish and fanciful, my
child?' he asked, gently.

'Please don't call me your child!' she snapped, seeking
to hurt him as he had unknowingly hurt her. She must
remember that she hated the man. That love and hate
were akin was beside the point.

'Ah, yes!' he mocked. 'But you called yourself a
foolish fanciful child, remember? Am I not to be
accorded the same privilege?'

'That's different!' she said, wishing he would move
away. That she had legs and could just as easily move
away from him escaped her notice at that moment. In
any case, her legs were incapable of movement. They
were turning to fluid and were about to give way when
they received support from an unexpected quarter. Max
Barrington's arms steadied her as his dark head bent to
hers, and his mouth met her unresisting one.

This was heaven! The kiss went on and on, then the
delicate, surgeon's fingers, moved over her body, gently
caressing her breasts. Ros moaned, knowing in her heart
how wrong this was. It was madness. Yet he belonged to
another and this might be the only chance she would
have to be in his arms. However fleeting the happiness,
she would snatch it while she could.

His hands cupped her breasts as he bestowed one last,
lingering kiss on her eager mouth, then he drew back,
letting his hands slide down her body to her hips. There
they stayed, warm and sensual, while poor Ros struggled
to bring her emotions under control. Tears appeared
from nowhere and streamed down her face as she forced
her eyes to meet his. His dark eyes were mocking,
cynical, and she had no difficulty at all in hating him

anew. That she might also love the man she refused to admit.

Max Barrington was playing with her affections, enjoying her confusion. No doubt he and his wife would have a good laugh about it later.

CHAPTER FOUR

ABRUPTLY Max Barrington turned away, giving Ros a
chance to wipe her eyes. The look she gave his broad
back was a savage one. He was hateful! And not a word
of apology from him, either.

He pushed long fingers through his dark hair, then
swung around to face her, eyes cold and expressionless:
'What are you doing about lunch?'

'W . . . what?' she murmured, hardly believing her
ears. To talk about food after all that had passed between them!

'Lunch. Food. A mid-day meal,' he went on, patiently. 'You do eat lunch?' he queried, standing much too
close for comfort.

'Oh, yes,' she agreed, weakly. 'I've brought sandwiches. Would you care for one? I mean there's enough
for both of us,' she hurried on, not really wanting him to
stay yet not wanting him to go, either.

'No, thank you,' he said, distantly, and an annoyed
flush crept up her face.

'Then I'll be getting on,' she said, equally distantly,
bending to gather up her brushes and bucket.

'After you have washed your face I will take you to
lunch!'

'What!' Ros straightened up, her mouth open in
astonishment.

'Here, borrow this.' Mr Barrington thrust a spotless
white handkerchief at her, and Ros stared at it wondering what she was expected to do with it.

With an exasperated sigh he took it from her and proceeded to wipe her face, very gently, much as he might do to his daughter. 'There—I think that will do. We are already very late.'

Ros still stood, rooted to the spot with amazement as, with a masterful gesture, the surgeon smoothed back damp tendrils of hair from her face, released her hair from the rubber-band which she'd used to tie it back, then tucked her checked blouse more firmly into the waistband of her slacks. 'Come, I have a busy afternoon.'

Gently he propelled her towards the door, locking the house behind him. She opened her mouth to protest but closed it again. Being cared for in this way was a new experience for the independent-minded Ros and she wasn't sure yet if she liked it. One thing she did know— Max Barrington was different from any man she'd met before!

'Please! Mr Barrington, it is nearly two o'clock,' she protested as she was neatly packed into the passenger seat of the bronze Jaguar. 'We won't get any lunch now. They finish serving at two.'

Max Barrington set the car in motion, and with a wry smile Ros settled back. No use trying to reason with the man. He must always be right. Let him find out for himself that there would be no restaurants open.

Of course he found one that served meals all day. He would! The restaurant was part of a departmental store in the town and Ros didn't feel so conspicuous in her casual clothes because the restaurant was full of shoppers and holiday-makers.

She hadn't realised until then just how hungry she was and the sandwiches would not have been adequate. She did full justice to the simple meal of ham salad followed by a large slice of blackcurrant cheesecake. The consultant had the salad but no pudding, and she eyed him, enquiringly.

'I have a busy afternoon at work,' he answered her unspoken query, and she nodded. He was having just a short break from theatre.

Mr Turner always insisted on having a lunch break away from the hospital. No sandwiches and coffee in Sister's office for him. Ros was glad Mr Barrington felt the same way. She longed to question him about Mrs Moran who had been on the morning list, but if he hadn't guessed that his co-owner and the junior staff nurse were one and the same, she certainly wasn't going to tell him.

'Thank you, Mr Barrington,' she said, as she reluctantly pushed her plate away. 'For the meal, I mean.'

'Ah, yes, the meal,' he said, blandly, and Ros clenched her fists then hurriedly pretended she had cramp in her fingers as his dark eyes followed the movement.

'Have you got time to take me back to . . .' she began, then stopped. He would wonder where she lived and she couldn't tell him she lived at St Ann's.

'To the cottage, you mean?' He rose, a tall, handsome figure, and tucked her arm through his as they walked to the cash-desk. Several pairs of interested female eyes were turned towards them as they walked, and Ros felt proud to be escorted by such a strikingly handsome man, even if it was strictly business.

'I . . . I think I've finished at the cottage, but if you could drop me somewhere near Ilton Market . . . But perhaps you aren't going that way?' she added, knowing quite well he was.

They strolled side by side to his car. Despite her height she felt petite and very delicate beside him. It was a pleasant feeling. To be protected, cherished, loved, by such a man. That would be wonderful, she reflected, wistfully, but such romantic dreams were a waste of time. Anyway she barely knew the man and didn't particularly like him. No, she definitely didn't like him.

'Where do you actually live?' she asked.

'We rent a small cottage near Brandon. But it is too small—no room to breathe,' he added.

He said 'we' rent a cottage. The three of them, a family group, Ros thought, sadly. The petite, curvy blonde, the darkly dynamic surgeon and their pretty little girl. She sighed, then pulled herself up sharply. 'I thought you might want to live at Fairhaven,' she said, unsure of his reaction, but he shrugged away the idea.

'It did occur to me, but it is no longer feasible,' he said, bleakly, and she glanced at him, gold-tipped lashes shielding her expression. She longed to know why it wasn't feasible but evidently he did not intend to explain.

Her bemused gaze took in the strong brown hands on the wheel of the powerful car. The dark stone in his heavy signet-ring winked back at her, and she glanced away. Nearly at Ilton Market. She could walk to St Ann's if he put her down in the town centre. Then he would speed on his way to the hospital, little knowing she was making her own way there.

A lump came into her throat and she swallowed nervously. She felt sad yet could not understand why. He was simply returning to the operating theatre, he wasn't vanishing from her life for ever. Why, she would see him the following Monday! Yet between now and then the weekend stretched away. He would be off-duty taking his family out, most likely. Perhaps he might take Mrs Barrington to the theatre in Ipswich, or further afield. They might even drive down to London and take in one of the West End shows, while a neighbour looked after Anne-Marie. Then to dinner and finally on to a club, where the elegant Mrs Barrington would fit snugly into his arms as they drifted slowly in time to the sensuous music . . .

'Miss Hayward!'

'Oh! Yes?' Mentally she shook herself. She had been lost in a dream world—a world of which she could never become a part.

'We are here. I will put you down outside Woolworths. Is that convenient?' Dark, dark eyes honed in on hers, and she couldn't think straight for a moment. She was caught in that searchlight again.

'Yes, yes, that's lovely,' she murmured. If he had suggested putting her down in the river she would have said much the same thing!

Max Barrington leaned even closer, his dark face only inches from her own. She was right, his eyebrows *did* meet in the middle, so her Cheshire Cat dream wasn't far out. They were lovely brows, she thought, absurdly, resisting the desire to run her finger along their length then down the side of his broad, straight nose, then across that sexy mouth . . .

'If you should decide at any time to sell Fairhaven, Miss Hayward, I would be pleased to buy it from you,' he was saying, but his words came from far away and she wasn't concentrating, anyway.

'Your eyes are glazing over, Miss Hayward,' he went on, briskly, and she opened her mouth in horror, warm colour flooding over her body as well as her face.

The wretched man must realise the effect he was having on her! And he was enjoying it, he must be.

'I can see how weary you are after your morning's

exertions,' he carried on blandly, and Ros mentally apologised to him.

Of course he couldn't know. He wasn't a psychiatrist, he couldn't look into people's minds. Or could he? Those brilliant black eyes didn't miss a thing!

Max must also be weary after *his* morning's exertions and Ros longed to smooth away the lines of fatigue, kiss the sadness from his eyes.

He got out and opened the car door for her while she was still trying to work out how it opened. 'There. We must meet again, Miss Hayward. To sort matters out,' he added, as she stared blankly. 'When will you be at the cottage again?'

Ros made a rapid calculation. Her days off the following week were Tuesday and Wednesday. At least they ought to be, but if Sister Ray wasn't well again she would have to work on her days off. 'I hope to be there on Tuesday, sir,' she said, unthinkingly, then heard his sharp intake of breath. She had called him 'sir' again! 'I want to get the carpets down and shampooed before the furniture arrives.'

He nodded. 'Your employer must be very accommodating, Miss Hayward. Giving you time off in the week,' he commented, and Ros bit her lip, unwilling to lie but unwilling to admit she was a nurse.

He didn't wait for any comment though, and before Ros could think of some non-committal remark, he was gone, manoeuvring the big car out into the traffic. She stood and watched until it disappeared from view. Then, sick at heart, she made her way towards St Ann's.

On the Sunday, Sister Ray returned to duty and Ros heaved a sigh of relief. Of course for the most part Jessie had been in charge of Jevington during Sister's frequent periods of sick leave, but when she was off-duty it was Ros' turn to carry the heavy responsibility. It had been so on the Saturday, though only from lunch until five.

Sister Ray's hair was liberally sprinkled with grey but she could not, Ros judged, be more than forty-four or so. She looked far from well, as she and Ros strolled together to the ward early on Sunday morning, having met in the lift.

'If I keep saying "welcome back" Sister, I mean every word of it,' Ros said, only half-joking, and Alice Ray shot her a sharp look.

'It's nice to be missed,' she commented, with a wry smile. The lift doors clanged to behind them as they got out. 'But I might have to go off sick again. I have to wait a month to see if things settle down, then it's back to see the gyny-man,' Sister added, and Ros' eyes darkened in concern.

'I'm sorry,' she murmured. 'I thought you didn't look all that well but I didn't like to say.'

Sister Ray shrugged, then walked tiredly towards her office, leaving a worried Ros to hang up her cloak in the staff-room. Sister had a lot of gyny problems according to Jessica, and would probably need a hysterectomy. Like many women she fought shy of such a step even though her child-bearing days were nearly over. She was a widow with a teenage son. Jessie thought she was going steady with one of the admin staff and Sister perhaps felt part of her attractiveness would go once she had the operation.

Ros could understand how she felt, though at twenty-one it was difficult to imagine herself as forty-plus. It wouldn't be right for her to persuade the older woman to have the operation even though Sister might feel ten years younger afterwards. It needed someone older.

Someone such as Mr Barrington perhaps? No, definitely not. Sister would be embarrassed. Ros shook her head as she hurried towards the office. They must hear the report then Sister would say good-morning to the patients while Ros organised the ward for the day, Sister having already said she would leave much of the work to Ros on this first day.

The feeling that Max Barrington could persuade Sister Ray to have the very necessary operation persisted and Ros found herself mulling over the idea whenever work permitted that Sunday morning. Because it was a weekend the ward work was kept to a minimum. In the afternoon the visitors would keep the ladies happy while the students settled down to study and the other staff relaxed a little.

Unfortunately the only student on the ward that day was Leonora Atkins, and Ros mentally crossed her fingers that no harm would come to the patients because of some misdemeanour of the willing but careless student.

Mrs Moran had survived her operation but was so poorly she was in intensive care. Ros wondered how Max Barrington felt about that, a patient he'd operated on being so ill afterwards with the threat of death hanging over her. She supposed it was all in the day's work for a surgeon—some you won and some you lost. Yet, despite his apparent cold, unfeeling attitude, she felt he genuinely cared for his patients and would be upset whenever he lost one.

She willed Mrs Moran to live and vowed she would phone ITU every day to see how the woman was. She had been so uncomplaining, so willing to accept whatever treatment, whatever medication had been proposed, and Ros missed her. Although surgical patients did not stay on the ward all that long, it was possible to become fond of them, of some of them, at least.

A patient of whom Ros found it hard to be fond was Mrs Tyler, a tall, obese woman in her late thirties. She was due for investigative surgery on the Tuesday but had a history of heart trouble and Ros didn't think Mr Barrington would be any too pleased. Her symptoms were vague to say the least, and Ros wondered whether they were genuine. At any rate Mrs Tyler was delighted to be there and enjoyed having the nurses at her beck and call, Nurse Atkins particularly.

Sister Ray broke into Ros' train of thought. 'Thank goodness it's nearly lunch! *And* we aren't on "take" this weekend,' she added.

Ros nodded. The surgical wards took turns at being on 'take' so as to share out the work between them. It was Fenner ward's turn for emergency admissions. 'Mrs Tyler, Sister. What do you think of her?'

Sister pursed her lips, then leaned back in her chair, exhaustion in every line of her. 'I really don't know, Ros. There probably *is* something there. And she's had all those children, too. I think she ought to be on Gyny. What Mr Barrington will say, I cannot imagine.' She closed her eyes, and Ros started forward, anxiously.

Then Sister's eyelids fluttered open and she gave Ross a wan smile. 'Don't fuss, my dear. I simply need a few minutes' rest. Go and see if the lunches are coming.'

They were. The porter brought in the heated trolley just as Ros left the office. Knowing Sister wouldn't want to be bothered unless it was necessary, Ros began handing out the trays. At St Ann's, food came up in individual dishes. Patients could, within limits, choose their own food. They were told what sort of diet they were on then left to choose a suitable menu, subject to Sister's approval.

Mrs Tyler was on a light diet, but her choice was unsuitable Ros noted with a frown, wondering how scrutiny of her menu had been overlooked. There was so much paperwork to be done that it was no wonder something occasionally slipped through the net.

The meal must go back. Ros let the nursing auxiliary help her give out the meals and sent Leonora Atkins to telephone the kitchen and ask for a more suitable meal for the overweight Mrs Tyler.

Of course it hadn't arrived by the time the other lunches were served, and Mrs Tyler wasn't slow to complain. She crooked a large, fat finger at Leonora, who trotted willingly over, only to be met by language so foul that Ros' ears turned pink. She'd heard some bad language in her time time but never so much of it in one go!

Reluctant to call Sister Ray, Ros walked briskly over in her best staff-nurse manner. Mrs Tyler's little piggy eyes glared, but Ros refused to be intimidated.

'Your meal will be along very shortly, Mrs Tyler,' she said, firmly. 'I know how hungry you must be, but . . .'

'You can't possibly know how hungry I am!' the fat woman snapped. 'You don't need half the food I do. Why, you're a skinny little thing and no mistake!'

Then her small eyes stared past Ros, who swung round thinking the woman's lunch had arrived. Max Barrington stood just outside Sister's office, arms folded, his handsome face expressionless.

Ros closed her eyes for a second, then murmured 'excuse me' to the patient, but before she could walk away the woman grabbed her arm, her strong, work-roughened fingers digging into Ros' slender arm.

'Another thing, Miss Staff Nurse! You're too young to be running around giving orders, taking care of we sick 'uns! Where's that Sister of yours, that's what I want to know!' Her voice rose and Ros longed to be invisible.

Out of the corner of her eye she saw the surgeon approaching. Mrs Tyler's fingers took a tighter grip on her arm and Ros wished she could scream and shout too, just to relieve her feelings.

Making a superhuman effort she prised herself free, and, keeping her voice and manner polite, assured Mrs Tyler her lunch would be there very shortly. She didn't remind the woman that the fault was entirely her own. She could appreciate that such a big woman would eat as many calories as she could get.

Ros' arm felt sore and tender where Mrs Tyler's nails had dug in but she knew she would shortly feel worse after the arrogant Mr Barrington had ground her into the dust!

They met in the middle of the ward, Ros determined to get her word in first, but he forestalled her: 'I want to examine Mrs Tyler. Please come with me, Staff Nurse.' His tone was brisk but not unfriendly and Ros took heart from it.

When Mrs Tyler saw the tall, good-looking consultant she was only too willing to co-operate, even calling Ros 'my dear'! She managed to complain about her missing meal, though, and Mr Barrington gave Ros a questioning glance.

Ros explained that the wrong meal had been sent up and that the correct one was on its way and once Mr Barrington relayed the message to Mrs Tyler, she appeared satisfied.

'Whyever didn't you say so, Staff Nurse!' she trilled. 'Here's poor me getting all het up and I'm that hungry.

I'm *ever* so hungry, sir,' she told the surgeon. 'They give me such *small* helpings! Not enough to feed a sparrow,' she carried on, with a sly look at Ros who managed to control her temper remarkably well.

'The meals, my dear lady, are intended for *sick* people,' Max Barrington said smoothly, to Ros' delight. 'People who are unwell seldom *want* a big meal.'

With a courteous word of thanks for the patient, Mr Barrington walked briskly away and Ros hurriedly drew back the bed-curtains and went after him, leaving the subdued patient to work out the meaning of the surgeon's remark.

Ros caught up with him just as he opened the office door and was about to follow him when he said, crisply: 'I will not require your services, Staff Nurse. No doubt you will attend to Mrs Tyler's meal.' With that, he closed the door firmly, leaving an annoyed Ros to return to the trolley and wait until she could serve the puddings.

Once or twice she glanced towards the office. She saw Mr Barrington's head and shoulders outlined for a second then he apparently sat down and she could just see his head. Of Sister Ray there was no sign, but she may have been at the filing cabinet, out of sight of the observation panel.

Poor Sister Ray! Ros hovered around anxiously, as the patients finished eating. Mrs Tyler's meal arrived at length and Ros took it over, to be met by a sullen silence. She saw the trolley off the ward, then she and Leonora settled the ladies down for their afternoon rest, a short rest because visiting started at two. She sent the nursing auxiliary to lunch, wondering if Sister wanted to go to first lunch as well. Leonora Atkins would have to wait until the afternoon shift arrived. So, too, must Ros.

At least the query about staff meals gave her an excuse to tap on the office door, and enter, her question already hovering about her lips.

Then she stopped, nonplussed. Sister Ray was sitting at the visitors' side of her desk, head bent, hand covering her eyes. Mr Barrington was perched on one corner of the desk, looking down at her.

Ros paused, uncertainly. 'I . . . I'm very sorry, Sister. Please excuse me, sir,' she murmured, as the surgeon lifted dark eyes to hers. 'I wondered if Sister wanted to go to first lunch?'

Sister Ray glanced up and Ros could see she had been crying. That man must have been blaming her for the fuss over Mrs Tyler!

Ros could feel the adrenalin flowing as she prepared to do battle for a ward sister she had come to like, but something in her manner must have warned the surgeon, because he smiled. True, only a brief flicker of smile crossed his face, but it made Ros pause.

'Sister is not well, Staff Nurse. She will go off sick now, I think. I understand a senior enrolled nurse will be on duty this afternoon?'

'Yes, sir. I shall be on until four-thirty,' Ros said, warily. 'Then the SEN will . . .' she paused, knowing he would object. 'The SEN is in charge until a staff nurse comes on at eight.'

'Aha!' He pounced on that, as she knew he would. 'I cannot permit this!' He emphasised the point by slamming one large fist into the other, causing Sister Ray to flinch. 'This ward must always be in the care of an experienced staff nurse. Always!' He glared at Ros as if the omission was her fault.

'It generally is, Mr Barrington,' Sister Ray spoke quietly but decisively. 'It is Sunday, however, and we aren't on "take"' so that staffing arrangements are adequate.'

Sister and surgeon traded glances, while Ros hovered, waiting to strike a verbal blow in Sister's defence, if necessary.

The surgeon won that round on points. 'The system must be changed,' he argued, stubbornly. 'Is there no other staff nurse who could be produced from a hat?'

'I could take an hour's break after the visitors have gone, sir,' Ros put in, eager to help. 'Then I could come back on duty until eight or so.'

Dark eyes assessed her, and evidently found her wanting, for he shook his head, and Ros flushed.

He didn't believe she could cope. It was there in his eyes, his demeanour. He simply had no faith in someone so newly qualified.

'We *are* chronically short of nurses, Mr Barrington,' Sister put in, quietly, her eyes warning Ros not to interrupt. 'I feel better now and will be better still for a spot of lunch. Staff Nurse might go off-duty after lunch then come back for the late shift.'

Again Max Barrington shook his head. 'I want a more experienced staff nurse. An *older* woman,' he added, tight-lipped and it was as much as Ros could do to keep quiet.

No good came of arguing with seniors. A consultant must be obeyed. Only Sister had the right to gently put him in his place and she didn't seem to be having much luck!

'Perhaps Miss Merry can sort something out,' he went on, thoughtfully, and Sister raised a brow.

'It *is* Sunday, sir,' she pointed out in her gentle way. 'One does not expect to see consultants on the wards on a Sunday, and certainly not a Principal Nursing Officer.'

For a second the arrogant Mr Barrington looked discomfited and Ros should have been pleased but for some unaccountable reason, was not. Perhaps there had been trouble at home, or an emergency on the men's ward might have brought him back.

'I came because of Mrs Tyler,' he said, to Ros' surprise. 'Everett Scott telephoned me at home.'

'Did he?' Sister couldn't hide her surprise, and Ros leaned forward expectantly, wondering why Mrs Tyler was of such importance that a consultant had to be dragged from his home on a Sunday.

Her curiosity wasn't to be satisfied, however, and he insisted on Sister going off sick, assuring her that he would sort out the staff problems.

Sister and Staff Nurse exchanged an amused, disbelieving glance. Mr Barrington must think he was a magician. Pulling a rabbit out of a hat might be easier than procuring more staff, particularly on a summer Sunday!

There was an uneasy silence in the ward-office after Sister Ray had reluctantly departed. Mr Barrington stood, head bent, seemingly deep in thought, and Ros hovered by the door, ready to take instant flight if he came nearer. That this was the man who, only days before, had kissed and caressed her at Fairhaven, she could hardly believe. *This* man was a tall, distinguished surgeon, autocratic, remote, very important. The man at Fairhaven had been a tall dark and handsome rake— no relation at all to Max Barrington, Esq, FRCS.

From under her lowered lashes, Ros stole a glance at his profile—the strong, determined chin, the . . .

Dark eyes met violet-blue head on, and she tried to pretend she hadn't been scrutinising his profile, merely waiting subserviently for his next orders! 'What do you want me to do, sir? About the afternoon shift, I mean? The other three nurses are due on shortly, but . . .'

Abruptly he cut short her faltering words. 'I will deal with it. Please attend to your patients.' He settled himself behind Sister's desk, pushed the chair back some way then, to her astonishment, put his feet on the desk, crossed his ankles and closed his eyes!

After one alarmed glance Ros bolted. Sitting like that he looked human—well, almost. The arrogant consultant she could accept and almost manage, but this was altogether too much.

Ros made sure the ward was as it should be and that all her patients were settled, and not needing attention, then put Student Nurse Atkins on her honour to hurry to the office if anything happened that she couldn't cope with. The report had to be ready for the afternoon shift, even though Ros hated returning to the office.

She tapped briskly on the door, then marched in, with a breezy confidence she was far from feeling.

Mr Barrington irritably waved her away and resumed his telephone conversation. Ros began to protest, then thought better of it. If he didn't want to be disturbed then the report must wait. Annoyed at being shut out of what was, at present, *her* office, she went back to the patients.

None too soon, as it happened, for Mrs Tyler had started again. Leonora Atkins worriedly beckoned Ros over.

'I'm sorry, Staff, but Mrs Tyler is poorly again,' she panted, blue eyes anxious.

Mrs Tyler was sitting up clutching her abdomen, emitting cries of pain. Bleating might have been a better word.

'What is it, Mrs Tyler? Was it the food?' Gently Ros

tried to prise the patient's hands away from her already distended abdomen, but met with surprising and determined resistance.

'I have to feel your tummy, Mrs Tyler,' Ros said, briskly. 'Please lie back.'

Motioning to Leonora to draw the curtains and wait outside in case any other patient needed her, Ros smiled at the obese woman. 'Tell me where it hurts,' she encouraged but Mrs Tyler lay back and closed her eyes. Then tears squeezed through her lids and came rolling down her cheeks and Ros gently wiped them away.

'It's nothing, Nurse,' she whimpered. 'It's just being here. In this *dreadful* place!' Her voice rose, and Ros caught the sound of quiet footsteps. They didn't belong to Leonora.

'No-one cares!' Mrs Tyler sat up and clutched at Ros' arm, the one she had already bruised. 'I could die here and none of you young nurses would notice! Too busy making up to that handsome Mr Barratt!'

'Mr Barrington,' Ros corrected automatically, then saw the black, highly-polished shoes stop just outside the curtain.

His dark head poked through the curtain. 'A moment, Staff Nurse, if you will,' he commanded. The head withdrew, but Mrs Tyler would not release Ros.

'Please, Mrs Tyler! I'll only be a moment and I will ask Mr Barrington to have a look at you,' Ros assured her.

'I don't want to be looked at, you fool!' Mrs Tyler bellowed, and Ros' ears burned as well as her face. 'I want something *done*!'

Ros almost lost her cool, for once. 'If you don't release me,' she said sharply, 'I cannot possibly *get* anything done for you!'

Her words had the desired effect, and Ros, with cap

askew and her arm hurting, almost flew down the ward to where the grim-faced consultant waited.

'Could you get someone to examine Mrs Tyler again, please?' she blurted out, before he could speak. 'She is complaining of abdominal pain again and the whole area is tender.' Ros was beginning to believe that a lot of the discomfort was in the patient's mind rather than her body, but the symptoms had to be reported.

Max Barrington made an impatient gesture. 'I have already examined her, but I will call the houseman. Why do you let patients have pains all over the place? You encourage them to have tender abdomens, knowing I am so busy!' he charged.

Ros caught her breath at the injustice of his remark. Encourage them, indeed! She could not let that pass, consultant or no consultant, but, perhaps fortunately, the afternoon shift appeared. At least SEN Baxter did, and Ros almost hugged her.

Mr Barrington, meanwhile, was on the phone again, while Ros, having instructed Leonora to stay within sight of Mrs Tyler but not to go within grabbing distance, hastily made a few notes for the handover.

All the while she was conscious of the brooding presence of the surgeon. Because he had commandeered Sister Ray's chair and most of the desk space, she had to make do with a tiny corner of the desk as she read out the relevant information, the rest of the afternoon shift having now appeared.

She and Sarah Baxter sorted out the afternoon schedule as Ros hadn't had time to write up the work-book. In that book each day's duties were fairly allocated among the various staff, some for dressings, one for theatre duty, one to write-up the Kardex, and so on.

On a Sunday there was mainly paperwork, and all the

relevant dressings had been done during the morning. Ros put herself down for visitor duties, dealing with their queries, etc. In addition she would oversee the ward until she went off duty, as she had no doubt Mr Barrington had been unable to produce the vastly-experienced staff nurse he so desired.

When she would get time to go to lunch, she wasn't sure, but it seemed unimportant. She might send some-one down to the canteen for a sandwich for her. It wouldn't be the first time.

A nurse was despatched to attend the doctor when he examined Mrs Tyler, Leonora Atkins was sent to lunch, and Ros would have relaxed a little, shared a joke with the SEN before the visitors arrived, except for the dark presence at Sister Ray's desk.

He had remained silent during the handover, and now Ros turned to him, enquiringly. She had no doubt whatsoever that he would have some complaint to make, some criticism. She waited with a resigned expression on her face, then found that she was watching his mouth, that beautiful, sensuous mouth. Hurriedly, she fixed her gaze instead on the filing cabinet behind Max Barrington's proud head.

CHAPTER FIVE

'You appear to have everything under control, Staff Nurse,' Mr Barrington said, almost affably, and both Ros and the SEN stared at him.

Ros recovered quickly from the unexpected praise, and murmured her thanks. 'I take it that you are satisfied with the staffing arrangements for this afternoon, sir,' she added.

'Yes, perfectly satisfied, thank you,' he purred, and Ros decided she liked him after all. Then he went on: 'I have arranged for Relief Sister Rosebery to come on at four. She does so as a special favour.'

As a special favour to the arrogant Max Barrington, Ros reflected, crossly. There had been no need to drag her in on what must have been her day off.

'Until then you will be in charge, Staff Nurse.' He bestowed a gracious smile on Ros, who stared back, stonily.

She would *not* have her head patted like some spoilt child! She hadn't been considered experienced enough before but now she was good enough to be in charge until the Sister arrived. Why not allow her to take over the evening shift as well? Getting in a relief Sister was a slur on Ros' capabilities and she wished she had the nerve to tell him so.

'You may go to lunch now, Staff Nurse.'

'I . . . I beg your pardon?' Ros stammered.

'Lunch,' he repeated, slowly and distinctly.

Fuming, Ros got up and walked out of the office, not

trusting herself to speak. In any case what was there to say? Thank you very much, sir, I could do with a meal? No, mere words were inadequate to express the message she wanted to get across to him—a thrown vase or two would convey her feelings better!

Assuring the SEN she would take the shortest possible break, she hurried down to the ground floor, scorning the lift. When she got to the canteen the queue was so long she decided it wasn't worth it. Hospital food was usually mediocre, very occasionally good, and she couldn't be bothered to find out which it was today. Usually Sundays there was roast beef and a rock-like Yorkshire pudding.

Aunt Gwen made delicious Yorkshire pudding, Ros recalled sadly as she slipped out of the hospital building and strolled across the carpark. Light and fluffy and . . .

Oh, what did it matter now! Aunt Gwen was gone and would never return. Hastily blinking back the tears Ros circled the big carpark a couple of times, waiting until the second lunch crowd had dwindled in the canteen. Then she would buy a sandwich or a packet of crisps and take it back to the Nurses' Home.

A few minutes later she took her cheese and tomato sandwich back to her room and sank thankfully down onto the small, hard bed.

It was a big, sunny room, much nicer than those allocated to untrained staff. It was an annexe of the main Nurses' Home which meant it was quieter and Ros could get a good night's sleep, which was not always the case in the main Home.

A good night's sleep, peace and quiet. Was that all she had to look forward to? Pensively, she bit into the sandwich, not really tasting it.

She was beginning to adopt a middle-aged attitude.

Early to bed, early to rise, her only excitement a weekly dose of Coronation Street on the box! Was that all there was to be in her life?

Unbidden, a dark mocking face floated before her. The Cheshire Cat again, masquerading as Max Barrington!

Her pulse quickened. Angrily she flung away the remains of the sandwich then had to bend down and clear it away. *That* was what she wanted in life! Max Barrington laughing down at her, gazing at her with tenderness, his sensitive hands probing the secret places of her body, setting her pulses aflame . . . That was what she needed! Not quiet evenings and early nights. If she had an early night she wanted to spend it in Max's arms with no thoughts of sleep!

There, she had faced it. The cold plain fact was that she was in love with the darkly handsome Max Barrington. No! She covered her face with her hands, her eyes filling with tears of frustration and longing. No, it wasn't possible, could not be possible. It was a stupid and dangerous infatuation, that was all. Some women might have considered *any* man fair game, even a married one, but that wasn't Ros' way. He was beyond her reach and the sooner she came to terms with the fact, the better.

Head held high, Ros strolled back to the ward. This afternoon she would immerse herself in work and put the surgeon right out of her mind.

SEN Baxter was at the end of the ward talking to a patient when Ros returned. The ward seemed quiet, as her gaze swept over the patients, mentally counting heads. Some would be in the dayroom, of course.

All appeared to be in order and Ros didn't bother to tell Nurse Baxter she was back. She would just have a

quick flick through the Kardex to see if any new entries
had been made.

Her eyebrows lifted in surprise when she saw Mrs
Tyler's case-notes on the desk and she hurriedly filed
them. Presumably Mr Barrington had been reading
them and no-one had thought to put them away afterwards. That would not do. Ros frowned, aware she
would have to speak to the nurses about the dangers of
leaving confidential documents where unauthorised
people could see them. Now she thought about it, Mrs
Tyler wasn't in the ward. Presumably her aches and
pains had subsided sufficiently for her to sit in the
day-room for a while. That was good news.

Her honey-blonde head was bent diligently over the
work-book when the office door was pushed open. Ros
raised her head, a smile ready for Nurse Baxter, but Max
Barrington strolled in, a tray in his hands.

Startled, Ros made room for the tray and for the
surgeon. 'I . . . I thought you had gone, Mr Barrington,'
she said, breathlessly. Now that she knew why her pulses
quickened whenever he came near, she was self-
conscious about it, afraid that his quick mind would pick
up the vibrations, and sneer at her gullibility.

'I had a snack in the kitchen. I saw you pass. Here,' he
handed her a cup of black coffee and stood over her,
milk jug raised.

'Black will be fine, really, sir,' she assured him, her
thoughts in turmoil. She hated black coffee but his
presence so confused and alarmed her that she couldn't
think straight.

As Ros was settled in Sister Ray's chair, he had no
choice but to sit at the other side of the desk, where he
frowned down at his coffee-cup.

Ros stole a glance at him, pretending she was staring

out through the observation panel. Not that she could see a lot unless she stood up.

Being Sunday Max Barrington had left off his week-day suit of dark grey complete with elegant waistcoat, and wore instead a light-weight suit in bottle green, his lighter green shirt unbuttoned far enough for her to catch a glimpse of that dark mat of hair. His face might have been carved from a dark marble, his Greek god features harsh, roughly carved, but the sculptor had gone to town on his eyes and lashes. Those deep-set brilliant eyes were shielded by enormously long lashes, dark and curling. He must have been a beautiful child, she thought, wishing she had known him then, though there was a lot of him in his daughter, blonde as she was—a smaller, trimmer version of his nose, similar dark lashes, a mouth that showed promise of being sensuous and appealing one day . . .

'I make no charge, Staff Nurse.' Anne-Marie's father had an uncanny knock of reading her mind, and the dark unfathomable pools that were his eyes bored into her.

Ros felt the warm colour suffusing her face but could do nothing about it. There was no point in pretending she hadn't been staring, but it couldn't have been that obvious, could it?

'I was wondering why you were still here, Mr Barrington,' she said, cheekily.

It was the wrong thing to say and his dark eyes snapped at her for her impudence. 'I am here until Sister Rosebery comes,' he announced.

'Oh! I could give you a ring when she comes, if you would prefer that?' Ros offered, wishing him miles away. He could not possibly want to stay on the ward, not on a Sunday and with his family waiting.

'No, Staff Nurse, I would not prefer that,' he said,

irritably, his lips coming together in a hard straight line and Ros wondered that she had ever thought his mouth sensuous.

'Oh!' she said again, then gulped down the unpleasantly strong coffee, and gathered the cups together as he had also finished.

He called her back as she was halfway out of the door. 'Where are Mrs Tyler's case-notes? Not mislaid, I trust?'

There was a wealth of meaning in his last sentence, and angry words trembled on Ros' generous mouth. 'I filed them away, sir. Someone . . . I suppose *you* left them on the desk?' Realisation downed and she didn't need his curt nod to confirm her suspicions.

'I'm sorry, sir,' she murmured, making her escape.

Why, oh why couldn't he leave her alone? Why must he sit there in silent condemnation? *Please* go away, Mr Barrington, she said silently, staring at the empty cups, *his* empty cup. She swallowed, then ran both taps full on.

She splashed the floor, inevitably, and was hunting under the sink for a floor-cloth when she heard footsteps behind her. Her upturned face was young and vulnerable, robbed of its usual mask because of the intensity of her feelings, and her lips were swiftly kissed—but not by her dream lover.

Everett Scott beamed down at her. 'You know, I could go for you in a big, big way, kid!' he joked, his voice loud enough to be heard in the office.

Scarlet, she waved him to silence, then wiped the floor, hoping Mr Barrington would not come to investigate.

'I've come to see the big black-eyed chief,' Everett went on in a hoarse whisper, then slapped her bottom just as she was getting up.

'Everett!' she stormed, her eyes darkening with pain

and humiliation. What if Max Barrington should see—
or hear? His nasty mind would put its own interpretation
on the horseplay!

'Sorry, sorry!' Everett grinned, big teeth gleaming.
'Usually you're so . . . so distant,' he went on. 'But
today lovelight was shining out of your eyes. How
could I resist such a vision? So I didn't,' he finished,
smugly.

His infectious laugh rang out at the cross expression
on her face and she could resist no longer. A slow smile
spread from her beautifully curved lips to her eyes.

'Why, when you smile you look almost beautiful!'
Everett assured her.

'Hm. I've heard that before. I expect you tell all the
girls the same thing!'

'No, no, I don't. I have a different package of sayings
and compliments for each girl—all carefully indexed,'
the registrar assured her solemnly, and Ros giggled.

'That's better! See, your Uncle Everett is good for
you. A dose of Everett Scott twice a week would work
wonders!' he quipped.

'Please go away,' she begged. 'Mr Barrington is in the
office,' she added, as he showed no inclination to hurry
away.

A heartfelt sigh was drawn from the depths of him.
'You just admit you love me then I'll go,' he promised,
tickling the back of her neck.

Aware that such behaviour ought not to be permitted
when they were both on duty, she treated him to one of
her special glacial stares.

That did the trick. Muttering under his breath,
Everett sauntered away, leaving Ros weak and trembling, not because she fancied Everett but because she'd
been so afraid Max Barrington would interrupt, make

some chilling, cutting remark. She could not have borne it.

She took her time returning to the office. Instead, she walked past the half-open door from where she could hear voices—Max Barrington's and Everett's. She waved to Nurse Baxter then strolled down the ward. Nearly visiting-time and already one or two early-comers were outside the ward compound, staring in through the glass panel in the swing-doors.

When she reached Mrs Tyler's bed Ros paused. Nurse Baxter and the nursing auxiliary, Ella Bolton, were making up the bed with fresh linen. Ros stood by the linen-skip, eyes questioning.

'Mrs Tyler has gone back to medical, Staff Nurse,' Nurse Baxter said, briskly, folding back the blanket and sheet to make an admission pack.

'Why?' Ros asked weakly, too surprised to be annoyed that *she*, the nurse in charge, knew nothing about it.

Sarah Baxter sent her a puzzled glance. 'I imagined you knew that a move had been arranged, Staff. Mr Barrington was shouting down the phone to him. That would be when you were at lunch, though, I forgot.'

'Shouting down the phone to whom?' Ros persisted. 'Mr Tyler?'

'No! Dr Thomas. Mr Barrington said Mrs Tyler should never have been admitted to his ward. It wasn't surgery she needed,' Nurse Baxter went on, keeping her voice down to a whisper, in case anyone else was listening.

'We ought not to be talking about a patient in front of others,' Ros murmured. 'But I must know. Come into the day-room for a second.'

Leaving the nursing auxiliary to finish off, they walked

into the small but sunny day-room. Because visiting-time was imminent, all the patients had now returned to bed or were sitting in chairs by their beds. Usually the day-room was full, as the ladies preferred to get away from their beds if they possibly could.

Nurse Baxter perched on the arm of any easy-chair. 'He was furious! Mr Barrington, I mean. Shouldn't want to get on the wrong side of him!' she added, with a chuckle.

Ros, who generally *was* on the wrong side of him, silently agreed.

'He's quite nice when you get to know him, though,' the grey-haired SEN went on, and Ros shot her a surprised glance. 'He actually smiled at me once,' Nurse Baxter laughed. 'Though his eyes are always watchful and sort of cold, aren't they? As if he's been hurt in the past and is afraid to let himself go. Afraid of a rebuff.'

Perhaps that was it, Ros mused. She had often been emotionally hurt as a child in the Home and before, when her parents died. Now she, too, couldn't unbend with people, afraid they might jeer and simply turn their backs on her. It could be that Mr Barrington had suffered similarly as a child, perhaps after he left his native land.

'Anyway, about Mrs Tyler,' Nurse Baxter was saying. 'Mr Barrington said she ought not to be on his ward. That was why he came in on a Sunday—Mr Scott phoned him. Said he wasn't happy about Mrs Tyler being admitted for surgery.'

'I see,' Ros said, with a calmness she did not feel. At least there was some plausible reason for the consultant to be on the ward. And he had remained until Mrs Tyler was transferred but surely he could go home now? She frowned. 'Do you think Mr Barrington is staying long?'

'He said until Sister Rosebery arrived.' The SEN winked. 'Might be something else he's hanging on for.'

When Ros turned puzzled eyes on her, Nurse Baxter exclaimed: 'Don't tell me you don't know about him and Monica Rosebery? That's common knowledge, Staff!'

'But the man has only just arrived! He can't possibly have started an affair already!'

'No, of course not, but they knew each other before— in London. She's his old flame! Could be why he buried himself here instead of staying at a teaching hospital,' Nurse Baxter added, darkly. 'Well, I must get on.'

She bustled away, leaving Ros white-faced and shaking. A beautiful blonde wife, and a beautiful auburn-haired mistress! What more could he possibly want.

'There you are, Staff Nurse!' a cold voice broke into her muddled thoughts, and her voice trembled as she murmured a polite, 'Can I help you, sir?'

'You ought to be in the ward office ready to deal with visitors' queries, not relaxing in here!' he snapped, eyes biting in their contempt. 'In my last hospital this would never have been permitted,' he added, unfairly.

'I was discussing Mrs Tyler with the enrolled nurse, sir,' Ros said with a calmness she was far from feeling. 'I would have appreciated being told of her imminent move,' she went on, reproachfully.

'I apologise, Staff Nurse.' Max Barrington's voice held no note of apology, they were so many empty words, but at least he had made the effort.

He gestured to her to proceed him, and they walked briskly back to the office. Ros could feel several interested gazes upon them. It wasn't often a consultant had to dig staff out of the dayroom, and it would be reported to visitors, who were now due to be let in.

'The visitors, Staff. It's time?' the third-year student,

Valerie Ives, said with a question in her voice.

But it was Max Barrington who nodded permission for the doors to be opened before Ros could collect her scattered wits. Her lips tightened. Now he was taking the ward from her!

And there was nothing she could do about it—nothing. She could complain to her Nursing Officer, and the complaint would go all the way up to Miss Merry, who apparently disliked Max Barrington anyway. But the PNO would not want to risk offending him. A mere staff nurse was as nothing compared with an eminent consultant surgeon. As always, rank had its privileges, Ros thought sourly. It didn't matter any more. She had taken so many knocks from the hateful Max Barrington that she reckoned she was becoming immune. Nothing else he said or did could hurt her now.

But she was wrong. Later, when the last of the visitors had departed and the other nurses were giving out the welcome cups of tea, Mr Barrington said, smoothly: 'Have you come to any decision about Fairhaven, Nurse Hayward?'

Ros' mouth fell open, and she clutched the filing cabinet for support. 'Fairhaven?' she asked, in a strangled voice.

'But, of course. Our joint legacy, Staff Nurse. Can you have forgotten so soon?' he asked, in evident surprise.

'No, of course not, sir,' she mumbled.

'Speak up, Nurse. I cannot hear you.'

'I said of course I hadn't forgotten, sir,' Ros repeated, slowly and distinctly. How could she forget Fairhaven and the interlude in Max Barrington's arms?

'*Will* you live there?' he went on, eyes narrowed.

Guiltily, she tried to avoid his searchlight stare. 'I

didn't realise you knew!' she blurted out.

'That the adolescent staff nurse and the tall, blonde Miss Hayward were one and the same? But, naturally!' He made a sweeping gesture with his hand. 'How could I not know?'

'Yes,' she said, stupidly, then tried to turn the conversation away from that embarrassing subject. 'Will Sister Rosebery be on duty all week, sir?'

'That depends. Tomorrow, when Miss Merry returns, I shall speak to her. You have the duty-list?' He held out a hand even before Ros had plucked the list from the wall.

'Here, sir. Sister Ray was supposed to be off next Friday and Saturday. I'm due off Tuesday and Wednesday, but I'm happy to stay on,' Ros added.

'No, no. You must take your off-duty. You are not so important that the ward cannot run without you,' he went on, nastily.

Ros gasped. 'Staff Nurse Bradley is on leave for two weeks now, sir,' she ground out, wishing she could tell him what she thought of him.

He drew his heavy brows together. 'Mm. That is a problem. We must consult Sister Rosebery. See what free time she has.'

'I expect she won't wish to do full-time, sir,' Ros said, carefully. 'Her little boy is still ill.'

He shrugged. 'She gives in to him too much. Now that she is a widow she should have more time to herself, more freedom. Yet she is a prisoner of that spoilt child.' He sounded irritated, and Nurse Baxter's words came back to her. His remark lent credence to the rumour that Nurse Baxter had repeated. Mr Barrington wanted Sister Rosebery to have more free time—to spend with him.

Sick at heart and with a feeling inside that could only be jealousy, Ros waited head bent, for Mr Barrington to comment on the duty-sheet or to tell her more about Monica Rosebery, but the oppressive silence continued, until he broke it to ask:

'Well—what about Fairhaven?'

She raised dull, anguished eyes to his: 'I can't afford to live there, Mr Barrington. It will be too expensive. Unless I could sub-let part,' she went on, half to herself. 'Jessie, Staff Nurse Bradley, that is, shares with two other girls. They are wanting more room, I know . . .' Her voice trailed off. 'No, it's too far—though two of them have cars.'

'No, it will not do. I have a better plan, Miss Hayward,' Mr Barrington said, almost gently, and she managed a weak smile.

'Anything would be better than selling Fairhaven, sir. It's my home,' she said simply, then saw that glacial expression creep back onto his face—the cold marble mask again.

'So you keep telling me, Miss Hayward,' he said, harshly. 'You must have a parental home, surely?'

Ros shook her head, causing her cap to wobble. Irritably she took it off and re-secured it with hairpins. 'No, Aunt Gwen, my mother's sister, was my only relative. That I know of, anyway. I was brought up in an orphanage—a Council Children's Home.' She shrugged away the unhappy memories her comment had brought back. 'Fairhaven is the only *real* home I remember.'

'I see. Then we must make some arrangement about it. Some permanent arrangement,' he paused, then went on: 'We might share it. I take it that your off-duty is usually during the week?'

'Sister Ray generally has weekends off, or so I understand. And Staff Nurse Bradley, being senior to me, has first choice after Sister, and generally has Saturdays.'

'Then there is no problem. We will share the house— and the week, between us,' he pronounced, dark eyes sliding over her, thoughtfully.

'You will live there at weekends and I'll live there during the week?' she asked, startled.

'It is a plan that will enable us both to live in the house, is it not? At the same time we will not be under each other's feet. We will, naturally, share the expenses,' he added.

Even sharing the expenses with him, Ros didn't think she could afford to live there *and* keep on her room in the Nurses' Home but did not say so. The chance of keeping Fairhaven was too good to be missed. Her face brightened, becoming almost beautiful.

'I would like that, sir!' she assured him, earnestly. 'I was hoping that the furniture could be moved in on my days off but Mrs Barrington might not want that, I suppose. I mean, some of the furniture is pretty old and . . . and not elegant,' she floundered on, aware that yet again she had displeased him.

'You are suggesting I purchase new furniture, Staff Nurse?'

'Oh, no!' Ros was shocked. Old though it was, each piece held precious memories for her. 'I just thought we ought to ask what she wants. Mrs Barrington, that is."

A sardonic gleam in his eye, Max Barrington said: 'There *is* no Mrs Barrington. Your vivid imagination must have, conjured up one from somewhere, but where? Ah, I have it!' he carried on, while Ros sat there in silent shock. 'You saw Danielle at the cottage and jumped the gun!'

'Jumped to the wrong conclusion, sir,' Ros corrected

him, unthinkingly. 'I did. I could see how much your daughter resembled her and I . . .' Too late Ros saw where her remarks were leading her. She had been about to imply that Anne-Marie was the daughter of Max Barrington and the elegant blonde! 'I mean, I thought they must be your wife and daughter,' she finished, miserably.

'Anne-Marie is my daughter, yes. Danielle is my wife—no!' he thundered, aware of the implications of Ros' unfortunate remark. 'Anne-Marie resembles Danielle slightly because Danielle is my late wife's cousin,' he went on. 'It is possible that I shall marry Danielle. My daughter needs a mother, but . . .' He broke off. 'That need not concern you, Miss Hayward.'

'I'm sorry. About my mistake, I mean. Is it all right about the furniture coming on Tuesday? I'll postpone it if you wish?'

'No, no. That will be fine. I will see that you have your two days off as planned, then you can prepare Fairhaven. I will stay there next weekend,' he added.

'Very well, sir.'

'What made you think I did not recognise you at Fairhaven?' he asked, a tantalising little smile hovering about his wide mouth. 'Was it because of your disguise of unpressed trousers and wind-blown hair?'

Ros gritted her teeth. 'I wore my oldest clothes because I was cleaning, sir,' she said, tartly. 'It wasn't meant to be a disguise. It's just that you were so, so different at Fairhaven.'

'Different? In what way?' he purred, leaning towards her.

'I . . . I mean you were kinder,' she floundered. 'Not . . . Oh, dear!' She tried to laugh it off but met with no response from the surgeon.

'You mean because I kissed you, I presume? You must not read anything kind into that, Miss Hayward. All women are alike,' he went on contemptuously. 'They offer and men take. I took only what was so freely offered.'

Ros' blood boiled. She couldn't take any more. He was impossible. If she didn't get away from him now she would wipe that sneering, condemning expression from his handsome face.

Burning with anger, she cast him a look of such loathing that he ought to have died on the spot, then hurried away.

CHAPTER SIX

Ros let out a sigh of pure satisfaction. Fairhaven was a home again. In the bright sunlight everything, inside and out, gleamed just as it had when Aunt Gwen lived there.

She stepped back, the better to see and admire. She was in the sitting-room, a pleasantly bright room which had once been two. Now, the rear overlooked attractive gardens full of roses and shrubs. The french windows led onto a small terrace with steps leading down to the garden. The front window did not have such a pleasing aspect for the front garden was tiny and consisted of a small patch of lawn, but there, too, Aunt Gwen's roses bloomed, a reminder of her presence if Ros needed one.

Blinking back what she considered as childish tears, Ros wandered through to the kitchen. It was rather small but everything necessary was there—the cooker with its rotisserie, an old but functional washer and spin dryer, plenty of work surfaces. She cheered herself with the thought that on her holiday she could spend the whole week here, just returning to her room at the weekend. She closed her eyes. Bliss, perfect bliss.

But there was still the thorny subject of money to be raised with her co-owner. He had said they must share expenses, but how much of an expense was it going to be? There was no mortgage but rates and heating bills must be paid. Then the roof needed retiling, according to Mr Barrington.

Never mind, something would turn up. Something always did. With that thought in mind Ros put her deck-chair where it would get most sun and relaxed, letting her mind drift. The hum of insects and the occasional chirp of a bird were pleasant. She could almost believe she was rich, a lady of leisure with nothing to do but sit around all day, her only problem being what to order for lunch. Naturally she would have several servants. She smiled. She must have a cook-housekeeper at least, then a maid. Perhaps a lady's maid as well? No, yes, why not? Then the gardens needed attention. But a part-time gardener would suffice.

She opened her eyes and surveyed the reality. The gardens *did* need attention. Sighing, she rose, a tall, graceful girl, like a daffodil in her green dress with her honey hair caressing her shoulders. She opened the shed and got out the hand-mower.

Minutes later she was wishing for a powered mower in addition to the tumble dryer and house full of servants she already craved. Mowing, particularly on a hot day, was hard work. And there seemed more lawn than she remembered, probably the early summer rain had helped.

While the house was empty, Aunt Gwen's handyman, Mr Dunster, had kept the grass and the weeds in order, but now that he was getting on a bit he'd told Ros he didn't want to continue. He was prepared to mow the lawns for the rest of the summer, he assured her, but that was all. Ros had volunteered instead, glad of the opportunity for saving money. Fairhaven was a white elephant, just as the solicitor had told her.

Funny, she hadn't seen Mr Simpkin since he'd brought her here in that lovely car. The day she met Danielle and thought her to be Max Barrington's wife.

No, she didn't want to think about Max Barrington. She must put him right out of her mind. To think he was

carrying on with *two* women! Sister Rosebery, when she
arrived last Sunday, had all but thrown her arms around
him. She'd called him 'Max, my darling'. In front of the
other nurses, too, Ros reflected, cross both with Sister
Rosebery and with herself because she could not put that
awful man out of her mind, try as she might. And she
wasn't trying very hard, she mused, a bitter smile flitting
across her face.

Wearily she trudged around with the mower, and was
only halfway through when she became aware that she
was being watched. She stopped, wiping the perspira-
tion from her eyes. Anne-Marie Barrington stood, hand
in hand with her father, watching with interest.

'Good afternoon, Mr Barrington,' Ros said, politely
but distantly, and the consultant inclined his head in
what she considered a condescending way.

There was nothing proud or condescending about
Anne-Marie. Eagerly, she skipped forward, offering to
empty the grassbox each time it was filled.

Ros willingly accepted, after an enquiring glance at
Mr Barrington, who nodded his agreement. With Anne-
Marie's help and friendly chatter, the task was consider
ably lightened, and Ros responded to the little girl'
unselfconscious friendliness. One day, she promised
herself, she would have a daughter like Anne-Marie.
Despite the quietness of her life, Ros expected that one
day she would marry and have children. Perhaps after
she had achieved her ambition and become a ward sister
She didn't wish to go further than that. She was content

That awful word again, contentment. She frowned
Of course she wasn't content. Not with the darkly
attractive Max Barrington so near yet so far!

'There, that's another job jobbed,' Ros said briskly
as the puffing Anne-Marie brought back the empt

grassbox. 'We can have a cool drink now, I think,' she added, and Anne-Marie's face lit up.

'A lemonade? Have you got some lemonade?'

'Well, no. It's orange squash, actually. Will that do?' Ros asked, gently smoothing back a lock of hair that was blowing in Anne-Marie's eyes.

'Mm. Or an ice-cream?' Anne-Marie put in, wistfully.

'I'm afraid I haven't . . .' Ros began, but the surgeon interrupted.

'I think I saw a shop selling ice-cream. I will buy some.' Without stopping to ask if Ros wanted any, he disappeared towards the gleaming, spotlessly clean bronze car, and Ros was left to entertain his daughter as best she could.

Of course the newly-filled swimming pool caught Anne-Marie's eye, and she gazed at it, eagerly.

'Do you swim, Anne-Marie?' Ros asked, wondering if Max would let his daughter use the pool.

'Yes, I can swim three lengths!' Anne-Marie assured her. 'I'll ask Papa if I can swim here. Shall I?'

'Yes, you had better wait. He might be cross,' Ros said, remembering just how cross he could be when the fancy took him.

'He's never cross!' Anne-Marie looked scandalised, big blue eyes almost accusing Ros of a falsehood.

Ros let that go. She and Anne-Marie certainly saw different sides of the man!

By the time Max returned, Ros had shown his daughter all over Fairhaven. There were four bedrooms, three of them double, and Ros assumed he would want her to have the single room. It had much the prettiest view, anyway, overlooking a small area of orchard at the rear. Orchard was hardly a fitting name for about a dozen fruit trees but it sounded good. The bedroom was simply furnished with white-painted furniture and cheerful red and navy curtains which matched the bedspread. Overhead there were exposed beams, and the ceiling sloped towards the garden.

It was an ideal room for a child and had been Ros' own room until she outgrew the space and moved to a larger front bedroom.

That was another problem to be sorted out with Max Barrington. Which bedroom did he want to occupy? They could hardly play musical bedrooms, Ros swopping her personal bits and pieces over because he wanted to use at weekends the same bedroom she used during the week. She hoped she might keep the room she had been used to, but supposed he ought to have first choice.

Why should he? her brain argued. It's *your* home, Rosalyn. Fight for it! Tell him which bedroom you are having. He has two others to choose from.

Put like that it made sense. As he was to be there only at weekends he probably would not care which room he had, anyway. But agreeing that she should have first choice and actually telling the surgeon were two different things!

On his return, with enough ice-cream to feed a dozen people, he seemed remote and stern, even more so than usual. Ros couldn't let her anger and resentment show in front of the child, but by her cold, aloof manner towards him she made it plain to the surgeon that she was displeased. At St Ann's they were staff nurse and surgeon. When he said jump she had to obey. Here it was different. Or if it wasn't, she intended it to be so. She and Max Barrington were partners, co-owners of a valuable property, and she was by no means going to be the junior partner. Shy and retiring by nature Ros might be but she was going to fight for her home.

After her strawberry ice-cream Anne-Marie announced that she wanted to swim. Frowning, her father told her she must wait for a while but could play by the pool.

No sooner the thought than the deed. Anne-Marie eagerly stripped off, showing that she had come prepared, with a bright red school-style swimsuit under her pretty dress. She produced a rubber swimcap, white covered with pink roses, placed her shoes and socks in a neat pile by her dress, then skipped away, singing to herself.

Left alone with Max, Ros fidgeted, uncomfortable under his probing gaze.

'You resent my being a co-owner?' he shot at her.

Whilst the question wasn't entirely unexpected, Ros didn't know how to answer, then decided honesty was the best policy.

'Yes, I suppose I do,' she admitted, toying with her spoon. They were sitting on deck-chairs by the back door, out of the full glare of the sun. 'It was my home—I lived here for some years with Aunt Gwen,' Ros added. She wanted to be fair to the man but surely he realised how she felt, having to share her home with a stranger?

He considered the matter, eyes narrowed, looking every inch the Greek god. Or Hungarian god, she corrected herself. She wanted to reach out and touch his face, imprint every feature on her memory, but instead sat quietly.

'I must make sure Anne-Marie is not getting too much sun.' He rose heavily and walked away, leaving Ros seething. Naturally he must see to his daughter, but not in the middle of what might have become an interesting conversation!

When he returned Ros' eyes were closed. A slight

breeze stirred her hair and Max tugged at the strand of hair that was blowing across her face. Ros sat up with a cry.

His dark, enigmatic eyes were on her face and for one heartstopping second she believed he might kiss her. But the danger passed. Instead, he stared out at the trees as if seeking inspiration.

'You wish to know how I met Gwen Liston?'

Without waiting for an answer, he went on: 'My parents fled Hungary in the Fifties. We left our home, our money, my pet dog. Everything!' He slashed the air with one big hand to indicate that all was gone, that there was nothing left of the old life, and Ros felt a lump in her throat. If she had suffered, so, too, had this man.

'My brother was killed. At least, we left him behind. He would not come with us,' he went on, harshly. 'Later we heard he had been killed. A car accident, some said. He was run down in the street.' He paused, and Ros held her breath, not wanting to interrupt him.

'When we came it was to this part of the country. First to London then on to East Anglia where my father was promised work by an old acquaintance. As a storeman in a civil engineering firm. He, who was an economist!' he spat. 'But it was work. Good, secure work,' Max Barrington went on, more calmly, and Ros marvelled at his control.

'My mother died of cancer but I think she would have lived. It was her broken heart that killed her. She was softer, gentler, and much lighter-skinned than my papa. Her hair was brown. Her mother had been blonde, she told me. So it is that I have a fair daughter.' He turned towards her, the anguish in his eyes plain to see, and Ros tentatively put a hand on his bare arm. Then she immediately drew her hand back as if she'd been burned.

He appeared not to notice her distress. 'I could speak good English so it was not so bad for me at school. But the ways of the English were hard to learn and many times I floundered and was jeered at for my foreign ways.'

When he was upset, Max Barrington's accent became more pronounced, almost guttural, and Ros could easily visualise him as a small, lonely boy, battling with strange customs, being punched and kicked and sworn at because he was a foreigner, someone not quite nice.

'I learned the hard way, Miss Hayward.' His words brought her thoughts winging back. 'I learned never to trust and never, never to love,' he finished, bitterly.

Ros let her violet-blue eyes speak her sympathy, and he leaned forward, almost absently, and patted her hand. It was a friendly gesture and nothing sensual could be read into it, but it began a chain reaction up her arm as nerve-endings jangled and jumped at the contact, passing on the message all the way to her heart.

'Your Aunt Gwen became my Aunt Gwen. My father was a colleague of hers and she came to our rented house many times. She befriended the strange foreign boy, made me realise that not all the English were against me. Many were not, of course. I met some kind boys at school, as well as the nasty ones. And we had understanding neighbours, but I carried an outsize chip on my shoulder. I decided that everyone was against me!' He laughed without humour. 'I didn't know about you then. I should think you were not born.'

'No, I'll be twenty-two in September,' Ros whispered, afraid by speaking that she would cause him to clam up again.

'And I am thirty-seven,' he told her. 'A very old, staid thirty-seven, no?'

Ros blushed. 'No! I don't think you're staid at all!' she

protested. Far from it, she added, but to herself. 'You have certain responsibilities, a certain style to keep up. No-one expects consultants to go around playing practical jokes, or slapping people on the back all the time. Consultants must have a . . . a dignity, otherwise staff would not have any faith in them.'

He raised a brow, then smiled in a way that made Ros go hot and cold. 'Dignified sounds very much better than staid, I admit!'

As if sorry he had shown Ros so much of himself, he became distant again but Ros didn't mind now. He had become human, had shown her the real Max Barrington, warts and all!

'That's an odd name—for a Hungarian, I mean. Barrington,' she said, slowly.

He shrugged. 'My surname was virtually unpronounceable, so my papa changed it to something English. I resented that, too! But now I am glad. And you?'

'I beg your pardon?'

'You, Nurse Hayward, what about your early life? It cannot have been easy living in this orphanage you spoke of?'

'No, it wasn't. I was a shy, diffident child. I . . . I suppose I reacted by creeping more and more into my shell. Even now I have no *close* friends. Jessica Bradley is probably my closest friend. She . . . she's on holiday this week—I wonder if you would mind her coming over one day, to see Fairhaven, I mean?'

'Of course not. It is your home,' he assured her, not sounding particularly interested either way. 'You must have your friends to visit, and I mine.'

Did his visiting friends include Sister Rosebery? Ros wondered. Not that it was any of her business. But she did long to know!

He rose suddenly and walked away, a tall, muscular figure simply dressed in cream shirt and fawn slacks. His shirt had the top three buttons open, Ros had been quick to notice.

Moments later, she heard Anne-Marie squealing with laughter, so at least he unbent as far as his child was concerned.

She would go and join them. She and Max Barrington had not yet fully discussed the finances and it would be put off no longer.

Anne-Marie was splashing about in the shallow end of the pool, and to Ros' amazement the dark Hungarian had also come prepared for swimming, and sat on the edge of the pool his lithe, tanned body clad only in brief black trunks.

Ros swallowed nervously. This man had a bad effect on her. Ever since she'd first met him he had never been far from her thoughts. And didn't she dream about him? No man had that effect on her before. She'd met a few boys, been out occasionally, but always there had been something lacking in the relationship, some vital spark missing. They had been casual friendships, nothing more.

Now she realised what had been missing. The vital spark she'd been hoping for was none other than Mr Max Barrington! There was nothing wrong with the other boys. They simply had not been right for *her*. *She* had been waiting for something wonderful, some knight on a white charger, and now he'd arrived.

And she had fallen hook line and sinker for her white knight. She had found what she sought—but at what cost? She could not have Max Barrington. The most she could expect, if he noticed her at all as a woman, was a brief and cheap affair. A casual interlude whenever he grew tired of Sister Rosebery or the beautiful Danielle.

All these thoughts ran through her mind as she approached, diffidently, trying not to gaze at him.

'You are not wanting to swim, Miss Hayward?' he asked, dark eyes cool, dismissing.

She shook her head, looking down at her dress. 'I'm not suitably dressed. Perhaps another day.' In fact, she had swum only that morning.

His dark eyes roved over her, but it was not an impudent stare, there was nothing in it to which she could object. 'I see no reason why you cannot swim, Miss Hayward. As for your dress, it is most becoming.'

Ros flushed with pleasure. It was the nearest to a compliment that he'd ever paid her. And probably that was the nearest she would *ever* get to a compliment from him!

'I had a swim earlier, really,' she assured him, then moved away out of danger.

Anne-Marie beckoned to her and produced a beach ball from somewhere. Ros obligingly threw it several times and Anne-Marie swam after it, whooping and laughing. 'Why don't you come in, Papa?' she called. 'I want to play!'

Her father slid into the water but that wasn't what Anne-Marie wanted. 'No, Papa! You must dive in, show Ros how clever you are. My Papa is very clever,' she went on, ingenuously, turning to Ros.

'I know he is, but I expect he is tired and doesn't want to dive.' Ros would have liked to see him do so but perhaps it would be as well if he didn't.

Anne-Marie's lower lip drooped. 'Papa dives in for Aunt Danielle. She dives as well, then we all play in the water.'

'Oh, good. That's lovely for you,' Ros managed. She had visions of the lovely Danielle floating on the water, being held against that manly chest, being kissed, her blonde hair streaming out behind her, tantalising Max, fascinating him . . .

Hurriedly, Ros made her mind go blank. She refused to think about them any more. The least she heard about Danielle, the better.

'She's going to be my new mummy,' Anne-Marie prattled on, each word like a knife in Ros' heart.

She could not escape from that name! Danielle this, Danielle that. She moistened her dry lips, then with an artificial smile pinned firmly to her mouth, she said: 'Congratulations, sir. On your engagement.'

There was a surprised silence. 'I was not aware of any engagement, Miss Hayward. Anne-Marie's remark was premature.'

'Oh? I'm sorry. I didn't know it wasn't official yet,' Ros rambled on, her false smile beginning to slip. If it wasn't official yet it did not mean that it was a lie. Anne-Marie must have had some basis for her remark, overheard words that perhaps she should not have.

'As my daughter is on Christian name terms with you, Miss Hayward, perhaps I might be permitted the same liberty?'

'Oh, yes. Yes, of course.' Ros' anxious eyes met his and she found herself floating. Not literally, of course, but she would have sworn that her feet left the ground, so intimate was his glance.

'I will call you . . . What sort of name is Ros?' he queried.

'It's short for Rosalyn,' she said, breathlessly.

'Yes,' he said, doubtfully, clearly not finding either name to his liking. 'I shall call you Rosalyn,' he announced, and Ros waited for his permission for her to use his first name, but waited in vain. Seemingly he was still to be 'sir'!

Swallowing her disappointment, she murmured 'orange squash' to no-one in particular then fled to the sanctuary of her kitchen. *She* was only a nurse. She wasn't good enough to call him 'Max'. She tried the name experimentally, letting it roll off her tongue. Max. It had a nice, masculine sound. She . . .

A car door slamming alerted her to the arrival of Mr Barrington's girl-friend. The petite blonde paid off the taxi as Ros watched from the kitchen window, then frowned, as if wondering what had happened to the red-carpet welcome.

Ros called to her from the window and received a regal wave in acknowledgment. Then Danielle disappeared round the corner, drawn to the poolside by Anne-Marie's shrieks.

So much for a cosy afternoon! Now she felt the interloper, like yesterday's newspaper, old news but interesting enough until today's plopped through the letterbox! Well, today's hot news had just arrived, and she must make the best of it.

She did not want to take out the tray of iced drinks and hoped the surgeon might come in for it. She could then make some excuse about dusting or preparing a room for Anne-Marie. Something, anything, to keep her away from the cosy little scene at the poolside. But no-one came. Possibly Max had not even missed her.

Of course he wouldn't miss her. How could he, when Danielle was there?

Ros felt she could delay no longer and, with a heavy heart, she trundled out the tea-trolley bearing a pitcher of squash, ice cubes, glasses, straws, and four portions of strawberry ice-cream complete with wafers.

The trolley made little noise but the glasses rattled and gave her away. She had hoped to slip up unnoticed. Instead she had to run the gauntlet of three pairs of eyes—two pairs blue, one pair black. All sat in silence as Ros approached and she wished to heaven someone would speak, even if it was only to say they didn't want squash!

'Ah, here is Miss Hayward with our refreshments.' Max Barrington broke the silence, his dark gaze on her face, compelling her to follow his lead. He had gone back to using her surname. No doubt Danielle would not wish it otherwise.

Ros' lips tightened, but she did not comment. Instead she served the orange squash, then offered the ice-cream around.

Danielle politely declined. 'No, I must not. My figure. It will spread!' she exclaimed, in beautifully-accented English.

Ros hadn't realised that Danielle wasn't English, though she ought to have been warned by the name. Her very French accent was enchanting, Ros grudgingly admitted.

Anne-Marie leapt at the chance of another ice-cream and had Danielle's portion as well.

'Please sit down, Miss Hayward,' Danielle invited, patting the chair next to her.

It was galling to be invited to sit down by one's own swimming pool but Ros smiled and accepted. Danielle was pleasant enough and because Ros was jealous of her and Max it did not mean that the Frenchwoman reciprocated the emotion.

Yet there were undercurrents there, rising to the surface from time to time as Danielle questioned Ros

about her work, her hobbies, her friends, and about
Fairhaven itself.

'This house. It is too big for you, no?' She turned big
eyes on Ros, who nodded, tightly. 'Then you might sell
your half to Max. No?'

'No!' Ros echoed, firmly. 'It was my home, Miss, er,
. . . I'm sorry, I don't know your name,' Ros was
annoyed both with the suggestion and with Max Barrington for not introducing her properly.

He stepped in as Ros floundered. 'I am sorry. I am
failing in my duty as host. Danielle, this is Rosalyn
Hayward. Miss Hayward—Danielle Dubois.'

Both girls smiled and Ros said, 'How do you do?'
politely. Not that she particularly cared at that moment.

'Miss Hayward lived here for some years, Danielle,'
he went on, smiling at his fiancée. The smile reached his
eyes, Ros noted, and lit up his face. He looked younger,
more the marble god than ever. 'We cannot ask her to
sell her home to us,' he added, and Danielle shrugged.

'No, no. Of course. I apologise, Miss Hayward.'
Danielle smiled charmingly at Ros, who did not, *could*
not respond.

She was grateful for Max reminding Danielle that
Fairhaven had once been her home, but now the idea
was in his head he could well decide it was an ideal
solution. Of course it would be an ideal solution, from
his point of view . . . And from Danielle's, but even
so . . .

She could not, she simply could not sell Fairhaven!
She loved every stick and stone. It was unfair!

'You are looking very hot and bothered, Miss Hayward!' Max broke in on her thoughts, and Danielle's
laugh tinkled out.

'I was thinking, Mr Barrington,' Ros said, distantly.

'Papa, can we all swim now?' Anne-Marie broke in, and her father nodded.

'You have somewhere I can change, Miss Hayward?' Danielle enquired, getting to her feet. 'See, I have brought something to wear!' She indicated the embroidered canvas bag she'd brought, then produced what looked like a white leotard but turned out to be a one-piece swimsuit.

Ros would have thought Danielle would wear a bikini, wanting Max to see as much of her figure as possible. But he had probably seen *all* her figure anyway, Ros thought, morosely. Certainly Danielle had an excellent shape. A bit top-heavy perhaps. And her legs were on the plump side. She did not have the benefit of an English rose complexion either, being beige-coloured, for want of a better word.

Aware that her thoughts were catty, Ros tried to be extra nice to Danielle, who appeared to take all compliments as her due.

'My swimming-costume, Miss Hayward—you like it?' Danielle asked, coming out of Ros' bedroom.

Ros had waited for her as instructed, in case she needed assistance, and now her mouth dropped open in astonishment. Danielle had been poured into the swimsuit. Or else it was made especially for her. She looked stunning, heavy legs or not!

The big round breasts were accentuated by the cut of the material and when Danielle leaned forward Ros had an excellent view of her magnificent bosom. No doubt Max Barrington would enjoy the view!

Now in a thoroughly bad mood, Ros led the way outdoors. She had intended to swim again but she had no wish to expose her slight figure to Danielle's interested gaze. Beside the Frenchwoman, Ros felt young, gauche and thin to the point of emaciation.

Danielle could not be more than thirty but probably she was younger. Max would like a nubile young wife, but not one as young as Ros.

Together he and Danielle Dubois made an attractive couple, Ros conceded, watching them stroll towards the pool. The beautiful people. She'd seen that expression somewhere. It meant the jet-set, she thought. The young, beautiful rich.

Max Barrington might not be rich, though. A consultant's salary was very good but he might not have other resources. Unless he took private patients?

She had no idea what Danielle did for a living. Very little from the looks of it. Perhaps she lived with Max and Anne-Marie. During the school holidays someone must take care of the child. August tomorrow, a whole month of summer stretching ahead. Ros' two weeks holiday were in the middle of the month, when Jessie returned.

She heard a splash, a ripple as Max cleaved through the air and hit the water. She forced herself to watch as Danielle did likewise. The divingboard was fairly low, as neither Aunt Gwen nor Ros had cared much for diving.

Two beautifully-formed bodies swam and floated. Laughter drifted over to Ros, who sat on a deck-chair. Anne-Marie sat on the side, her legs dangling in the water, just watching her father and mother-to-be as they enjoyed their swim.

Danielle called to Ros. 'Please come in! It is delightful. You are afraid, perhaps?'

Ros made a non-committal reply, wishing that some being would come along and drain the pool, leaving Danielle Dubois floundering on the bottom!

As Ros now knew the pangs of jealousy, she felt she must try to help Anne-Marie over them.

'Won't you come and talk to me, Anne-Marie?' she called, and the blonde child turned her head. Her direct stare was so much like her father's that Ros' heart missed a beat.

'What do you want me to say?' Anne-Marie was nothing if not polite, and she came and sat by Ros, smiling up at her and waiting.

'Tell me what you have been learning at school, if you like.'

Anne-Marie frowned. 'Sums,' she volunteered, her face clouding over, and Ros giggled.

'I never liked sums, either. But they're useful.'

'Yes,' Anne-Marie sighed. 'So my Papa is always telling me. He says I cannot be a doctor unless I am good at sums. So I try.'

'You want to be a doctor, like Papa?'

Anne-Marie nodded, her face eager. 'Just like Papa. Danielle says I could be like Mama but Papa got mad!' she added, then skipped away before Ros could ask any more. So much for getting to know Anne-Marrie!

After their brief swim, which was apparently all they'd come for, Max and Danielle didn't linger.

Ros almost bit her nails in frustration, wondering how she was to get Max to herself to broach the thorny subject of finances. She seized her chance when Danielle walked languorously indoors to dry and change, leaving wet footprints and drips everywhere for Ros to clean up.

'Mr Barrington!' Ros stood in front of the surgeon as he made to follow his girl-friend.

He had the courtesy to towel off first, so as not to leave a miniature pool everywhere. Yet, his chest-hair glistened and Ros could see droplets of water left there.

'Yes?' He waited, impatience in the line of jaw, his eyes snapping at her as they did so often on the ward. He must be anxious to help Danielle out of her swim-suit! The thought gave Ros courage, and she plunged on about the cost of keeping Fairhaven running, how much she was to pay towards the refurbishing he insisted on, and whether he wanted to take up residence this coming weekend.

He drew his thick dark brows together. 'At the weekend we are going away. To Paris,' he began, and Ros went cold.

Paris. Were they to be married there? She waited, hanging on his every word.

'After that we will be at my cottage again. Perhaps the weekend after that we will stay. But we must have the housewarming then, no?'

'Housewarming?' Ros faltered. No-one had mentioned *that* before.

'Of course. It is a traditional English custom,' he said, firmly. 'Danielle will wish to invite friends from Paris. You, naturally, must invite some of your colleagues. A young man, too, perhaps?'

Ros coloured faintly. 'No, there's no-one. At present,' she added, and he seemed surprised.

'A pretty young girl like you must surely have many admirers? I will ask Danielle to arrange someone for you,' he promised, to her horror. He went on to talk about the financial burden that was Fairhaven before Ros could tell him she didn't want Danielle's assistance in getting a boyfriend.

The arrangements were unexpectedly generous, and Ros was overcome. He intended to pay for all the repairs and alterations, plus rates, etc. All Ros needed to supply was her food when she came on her days off.

'But it will cost you a fortune!' she exclaimed. 'You're being far too generous!'

'I shall expect a good return on my investment, Rosalyn,' he said, his voice softening.

Before she realised his intentions, his dark head dipped towards her, his firm, sensuous mouth covered her own, and tremors shot through her.

Arrows of desire pierced her heart, her very bones melting as he held her against his bare chest. One hand was at the small of her back, pressing her against his hard thighs. With the other hand he gripped the nape of her neck his big hand almost encircling her throat.

Ros' knees went weak and her whole body burst into flame, ignited by this magnificent man. In one small corner of her mind some reason remained. She ought not to let him, should not permit these intimacies. But desire triumphed over reason, and it was Max who put her roughly aside, his face dark with anger, his breathing laboured.

'Again you offer yourself, Rosalyn!' he snapped, tilting back her head roughly. 'You are no better than my wife!' he stormed, thrusting her aside.

She heard him running up the stairs to join Danielle and his daughter. Ros looked down at her hands, which were trembling. She felt cold, chilled to the bone.

But it was anger that made her tremble. He thought he could kiss and fondle her whenever he wanted to. Then he had the audacity to blame *her* for letting him! She loathed the man and never, *never* would she let him touch her again!

CHAPTER SEVEN

'I SIMPLY will not take no for an answer!' Jessica Bradley could be firm when necessary, and Ros ducked playfully away.

'Please, Jessie, I don't want to go on the town! I've never been to a night club,' Ros added to give weight to her argument.

'Then it's high time you *did* do,' Jessie said, stubbornly. 'I know you enjoy your solitary existence, but you're too young to hibernate. Now you're landed gentry you have to make the most of it!'

'Hardly landed gentry!' Ros giggled, her eyes alight with good humour. 'It isn't a very big cottage, you know. Only four bedrooms.'

'That's enough. If I ever marry Brian I don't suppose we shall be able to afford three bedrooms let alone four,' Jessie said, wryly. She leaned back in the deck-chair by the Fairhaven pool, and sighed blissfully.

It was Friday. Ros was due on at twelve-thirty. Sister Rosebery was taking the morning shift, and Jessie had insisted that they spend the morning relaxing, chiding Ros for spending far too much time in her room at the Nurses' Home.

It was true, Ros conceded. She was becoming a real hermit, a recluse hiding from society. And why? She was young, she *needed* to get out and about.

'It isn't easy, leading the high life, I mean,' Ros ventured. 'It's all very well you saying I ought to get out, go to parties, dances, concerts. But it's no fun on my own!' she wailed. 'And it's no use your saying you would come with me,' she went on, before Jessie could butt in. 'You've got Brian. Let's face it, being a staff nurse doesn't leave one much energy to do anything except flop out in front of a fire and sleep!'

'True, true. You are still coming to the club with us, however. It kills two birds with one stone—I can take you out, and Brian can come too, so he won't be neglected. You'll like it,' she enthused, grey eyes lighting up. 'They have a gorgeous male singer sometimes. Then they have special guests one night a month. Last time I went it was Lena Zavaroni.'

'Yes, I like her, but I don't fancy all those weird groups,' Ros said stubbornly, and Jessie sighed.

'Give me strength! I'll make sure there isn't a weird group when we go, I promise,' Jessie assured her. 'You'll have to get a dress, though.'

Ros screwed up her face. 'I expect I've got something that will do,' she ventured.

'No! You buy yourself a new dress! Some exotic creation that will cause heads to turn!'

'Oh, Jessie, I couldn't!' Ros wailed. Her retiring violet nature was almost sick at the thought, but Jessie threatened all kinds of dire punishment if Ros didn't produce a new dress, so she had to give in.

But she had a stubborn nature. Giving in to her friend's demands did not mean she was going to appear in some backless, strapless piece of nothing! She didn't feel she had the figure for it, anyway. Visions of Danielle's magnificent figure, her generous bosom, floated by, and Ros clenched her fists. Why should she bother, anyway? There was no-one to care how she looked, what she wore. Max Barrington would not be the slightest bit interested.

He wouldn't know where she was going, so he couldn't see her. A little demon whispered in her ear that she *could* tell him where she was going and when. In a roundabout way, naturally. Just let the information drop casually.

The more Ros considered the idea the more appealing it became. Somehow she must let the hateful, loathsome Max Barrington know that she was off to the Sundowner Club. Let him make what he could of *that*.

There was no opportunity at first. Mr Barrington had a full operating list, most of them from the male wards, and Ros didn't see him until late Friday evening. He and Everett Scott walked in just when an exhausted Ros and Leonora Atkins where snatching a quick cup of tea in the ward office.

Sister Rosebery was supposedly off at five but she'd clucked her disapproval at the lack of experienced staff and said it would never do for Mr Barrington to find Ros in charge.

Ros had explained pleasantly but firmly that if she was never left in charge she could not possibly gain the experience the consultant considered she lacked.

Sister had shrugged and said Ros could take charge for two hours whilst she herself had a break. Two hours was better than nothing, Ros had conceded, hurt that since Mr Barrington's arrival no-one had faith in her ability to cope. She'd managed, been in sole charge some days, on the men's ward.

The Sister had come back on duty for a while, assuring Ros she would stay until seven-thirty, that Mr Barrington ought to be gone by then.

However, it was only seven and she'd disappeared. She didn't say where she was going and had left her cape behind so Ros assumed the woman would return. She had probably gone to chat to a colleague somewhere, perhaps gone to Accident & Emergency, where her niece worked.

A grateful patient had left a big box of chocs for the nurses, as happened often, and Ros was debating between the charms of an orange creme and nougat when an icy voice broke in:

'Busy, Miss Hayward?' Max Barrington strode in, followed by Everett Scott, and Ros sprang to her feet, almost knocking the report-book onto the floor.

Both of them moved to catch it, and Max's hand closed briefly over hers, causing her to snatch her hand away.

Replacing the book further on the desk the surgeon looked around for a chair, but Ros stubbornly refused to give him Sister's chair, indicating instead that the red-faced student nurse should provide one for him.

'Would you care for some tea, sir?' Ros asked, polite but distant. Since the episode at Fairhaven she hadn't spoken to him except when absolutely necessary. It hadn't been necessary often because Sister Rosebery was always there, trying to anticipate the surgeon's every whim.

He shook his head. 'Visiting time is not yet, I think?'

Surprised, Ros said: 'Not quite, sir. It's at seven but they gather about ten minutes beforehand.'

'Why not let them in if they are gathered?' he enquired, smoothly.

'I do, usually,' Ros admitted, with a quiet smile. 'But once a Nursing Officer carpeted me for it. Said rules were rules and seven to half past was long enough for sick people.'

'True, true. However, as so many are out there, you have my permission. It is six minutes to the hour. An extra few minutes time with their visitors cannot possibly harm the patients.'

Ros beamed, forgetting as she often did how much she disliked him! Rules were made for the benefit of the nurses and administrators, she sometimes thought, as she opened the glass-door and assured the visitors she hadn't made a mistake about the time.

'Don't want you getting ticked off, my dear!' Mrs Walker's mother chuckled.

'I have permission from on-high!' Ros answered, watching as they poured in. More than usual tonight, being Friday, she supposed.

Tomorrow would be a busy day, as Jevington was on 'take'—admitting emergency cases over the weekend. They had seven vacant beds. One they must keep for Mrs Moran who would be back shortly. She could have come back before but as ITU had vacancies Mr Barrington had asked for her to be kept there. She was still very weak, but the prognosis was reasonable.

She returned to the office to find Max Barrington in possession of Sister's chair and Sister's desk, so Ros took the chair he had vacated and balanced the report-book on her knee. She left the door ajar as there was bound to be at least one visitor with a query.

'Where is Sister Rosebery?' Max shot at her, eyes narrowed accusingly, as if she'd spirited the woman away.

'I . . . I'm not quite sure, sir. Probably in the treatment room,' Ros hedged, unwilling to tell him Sister was off the ward. Not that he would blame Sister, of course. 'Shall I look?'

'No, send one of the nurses. Sister ought to be here at visiting time,' he said, irritably, flicking through some case-notes.

He was tired, Ros noted with concern, before going in search of Leonora Atkins. But the student was already coming in the door.

'Oh, Staff! Mrs Walker's mother and husband want to see Sister but I told them she'd popped out!' Leonora's plump face was concerned. 'Shall you come instead?'

Max Barrington's face was a study. Mingled disbelief and wrath chased across it followed by that cold, bleak expression Ros knew so well.

'Where exactly *is* Sister Rosebery, Nurse?' He addressed his remark to Leonora, who glanced at Ros, eyes pleading for her to answer.

'Sister is still on the ward as far as I know, sir,' Ros answered, calmly. Turning to Leonora, she said: 'Would you please find Sister, wherever she is, and tell her Mr Barrington is asking for her?'

With a puzzled glance at Ros, Leonora did as she was bid. Ros sent up a hopeful prayer that Leonora would think to enquire at the next-door ward and, if necessary, telephone from there. That was a point. The student wouldn't know that Sister might be in A & E. She'd better warn her.

'Not you, Staff Nurse.' The consultant called Ros just as she was slipping through the door, and she turned an innocent gaze on him.

'You know perfectly well that Sister is not on the ward, so why do you prevaricate?' he asked, sternly, while Everett shifted his big feet uncomfortably.

'Sister did not tell me she was leaving the ward, sir,' Ros assured him, 'so I assume she is here somewhere. If she *is* off the ward then she can't be far.'

'She was in the canteen working her way through a cheese omelette and chips when last I saw her,' the surgeon continued, ignoring Ros' gasp.

'It would appear you have forgotten her whereabouts, Staff Nurse,' he added, and Ros' cheeks flamed. 'It is, after all, time for nurses' suppers so it seems reasonable that she should be in the canteen, does it not?'

When Ros couldn't find words, he exploded: 'Well? What excuse is your devious mind conjuring up? Tell me!' he demanded, and Everett cleared his throat, noisily.

'Sir, look, I know it isn't any of my business,' he began, and Max Barrington nodded.

'You are right. It is *not* any of your business, Mr Scott!' he said, giving the registrar a look which would have crushed lesser men, but Everett wasn't a coward as Ros knew. If consultants were in the wrong, Everett would diplomatically tell them, even at considerable risk to himself. Consultants had long memories and wouldn't forget junior doctors who answered them back. An irate consultant was a creature to be feared!

'Sir, if Staff Nurse says Sister didn't tell her she was going to supper, then she didn't,' Everett continued, and Ros could have kissed him.

The consultant's black eyes swivelled from one face to the other and he nodded to himself. 'I see. Thank you, Mr Scott.'

'Yes, sir,' Everett muttered, miserably, and Ros sat down and took up the report-book again, avoiding Mr Barrington's eye.

Silence reigned as the consultant wrote up some notes, Everett gazed out through the observation panel, and Ros began the report. What Mrs Walker's relatives wanted, she didn't know. Probably it was better to leave them to Sister, as the patient had been in only for observation. Her mother was a dear but her husband, a tough-looking bricklayer, had a chip on his shoulder about authority and had already told Ros she was too young to deal with his queries!

It was a crime to be young, Ros reflected, crossly, as she wrote. She would be glad when she was twenty-five or so. Or really old, fortyish. No-one would say she was too young then! She would probably be told she was too old!

Where would she be at forty? Still a nurse, she supposed. A sigh broke from her, and Mr Barrington's keen ears picked it up.

'Sulking, Nurse Hayward?'

'No!' she exclaimed. 'What have I to sulk about?' Indignantly she let him see she was hurt by his remark.

'Nothing, of course. Your young man makes excuses for your errors, so you should have nothing about which to sulk,' the surgeon went on, testily.

Everett seemed about to speak so Ros sent him a warning glance. There was no point in Everett getting involved further. Sister Rosebery would apologise to Mr Barrington for her absence, then treat him to what Ros called her 'man-eating smile' and he would be restored to good humour, putty in her hands.

Sister did exactly that when she returned some twenty minutes later, having had far longer than the official supper-break. 'Oh, Max, my dear! I *am* sorry! Have you been waiting long?' Without giving him a chance to reply she swung round on Ros and said, crossly: 'Why is Mr Barrington waiting, Staff? Surely you knew I would be in the canteen? I told you I was at supper.'

Everett raised a fair eyebrow, and Ros shrugged, gestures that Sister missed but the consultant did not. All the while he was speaking to Sister, his eyes were on herself and Everett, a shrewd, assessing glance. No doubt putting two and two together and making five, Ros decided. He was impossible!

It was after he had gone, presumably home to bed and Danielle, that Sister beckoned to Ros, who had just given Miss Marchant a pain-killing injection.

'Yes, Sister?' Ros waited patiently while Sister Rosebery drummed on the desk. Her fingernails were too long for a nurse, Ros noticed. Claws, talons, ready to strike.

Mentally shaking herself, Ros continued to wait, standing so that she could see out of the observation panel. Mrs Lal was trying to get out of bed again! Ros made a move but the nursing auxiliary was already there.

'Mr Barrington is displeased with you, Staff Nurse,' Sister said, out of the blue, and Ros gave her a look.

Sister's glance shifted to a point beyond Ros' head. 'I know it's difficult being young and looking younger. But he is a hard man to please,' she went on, fidgeting with the paper-knife. 'I knew him in London.'

'Yes, so I've heard, Sister,' Ros said, coldly, and Sister half-rose then sat back again, her face flushed.

'I have no doubt at all that you have heard a pack of lies, Staff Nurse!' she snapped. 'But I *do* know how to handle him. He says whenever he comes on the ward you are sitting in the office drinking tea or rummaging around for files. Or else cavorting in the kitchen with his registrar or that little fat Ahmed.'

Ros' temper rose. She was going to give Mr Max Barrington a piece of her mind, even if it cost her a job! He was . . . No suitable word came to mind, and she stood, simmering, while Sister Rosebery continued to chronicle Ros' bad points.

She couldn't blame Sister Rosebery. She didn't like the woman, who was inclined to sit in the office while the

nurse slaved away—a fault for which she was castigating
Ros! Despite that, Ros knew Mr Barrington had put
Sister in an awkward spot. She would want to keep in his
good books—therefore Staff Nurse Hayward must be
torn off a strip and, if necessary, moved from the ward.
It didn't take a lot of grey matter to work out that Mr
Barrington wanted rid of her, thought her inadequate
for the job.

'I hope you don't share Mr Barrington's views on my
abilities, Sister?' Ros put in, when at last the woman had
finished.

'No, no. I expect you are adequate.'

'Sister Ray thought so,' Ros said, stubbornly. 'I
haven't worked with her here except for a short while last
Sunday, but I was her third-year student on Glynde.'

Sister Rosebery passed her hand wearily across her
eyes. A strand of richly-coloured red hair was straying
from her usually tightly-controlled bun, and she fidgeted
with it while Ros stood, thinking dark thoughts about a
certain Hungarian.

'Mr Barrington is accustomed to a teaching hospital, a
hospital where everything runs like clockwork,' Sister
went on, but Ros interrupted.

'A hospital where he's treated like a little tin-god!
Well, he isn't! He's flesh and blood and has the same
weaknesses, the same faults as the rest of us!'

'Max has no weaknesses that I've been able to find.
Sometimes I think he's *too* perfect,' Sister said, in a
cynical tone, and Ros smiled, grimly.

'If he has put himself on a pedestal he has a very long
way to fall, Sister. Anyway, of course he has weaknesses.' Certainly he had, notably that he liked to kiss
young nurses!

'I hope *you* haven't discovered some of these so-called

weaknesses, Staff Nurse,' Sister Rosebery said, crossly, causing Ros to ponder.

Perhaps he and Sister hadn't been lovers in London, or since. The grapevine could be wrong. Just because he'd followed her to St Ann's did not mean he came *because* of her. He might have expected that Aunt Gwen would leave him something, half, perhaps even the whole of Fairhaven, and decided to make the most of it. Why, he hadn't had the courtesy to attend her funeral!

No, he had not! When she'd mentioned it to him, he said he was away on a course and didn't know about her death until too late. He didn't care about Aunt Gwen at all. It was an excuse. He simply wanted somewhere to live. He might have stayed in London otherwise. That was it!

The more her mind dwelt on the problem the more Ros decided she was right. Max had no real interest in Sister Rosebery. It was Aunt Gwen's property and money he'd been after! He was an opportunist!

When, tired and dispirited, Ros got back to her room, she wasn't alone long before Jessie arrived, with her boyfriend, Brian, a tall thin young man almost hidden behind a bushy moustache.

Company was just what she needed, Ros decided, as she made them coffee. Jessie produced some cookies she'd baked earlier and they settled down, Ros perched on the narrow, uncomfortable bed, Brian in the easychair and Jessie on a big scarlet beanbag by his side.

They were happy, Ros thought, a trifle wistfully. They looked right together, as if they belonged. Ros desperately wanted to belong, but only to Max.

Where was he now? She stole a glance at her wristwatch, not wanting the others to think she was dropping a hint for them to go. Ten-fifteen. What was Max doing now? She supposed Anne-Marie would be fast asleep, but Max and Danielle? They might be sitting cosily just as Jessie and Brian were doing, he in his armchair, the Frenchwoman curled up by his feet, her blonde head resting on his knee. She might even be on his knee, comes to think of it . . .

She felt tears welling up behind her eyes, and hurriedly averted her face, trying to make her coffee last as long as possible. She could not cry in front of her friends. How Jessie would laugh if she knew about the torch Ros carried for that hateful Max Barrington!

No-one liked him, except Sister Rosebery. And, she supposed, Everett Scott, who got on well with everybody. How awful to be so disliked, so isolated. It must be a lonely life for him, she mused. Funny, she hadn't thought about it like that. Hateful, fault-finding people must be lonely.

'Penny for them, young Hayward!' Brian teased, and Ros smiled her secretive smile.

'Leave young Hayward alone!' Jessie put in, severely. 'She belongs in a different world from the rest of us!'

Ros grimaced. 'A different world, but not necessarily a better one, I can assure you! I was thinking about Sister Rosebery.' She went on to tell her friend about the ward sister's remarks and about Max Barrington's opinion of her.

Jessie gasped, white with anger. 'He had no right! Nor did that shoe-licking Sister Rosebery, come to that. The nerve of them! If you are going to be a sister one day you have to know how to cope with the office work. *He's* got a secretary. He doesn't realise how much paper-work there is.'

'You're probably right, but nearly every time we've met, I have been in the office,' Ros conceded, 'so he imagines I spend all my time there. I don't know how he thinks the ward work gets done,' she went on, wearily, 'for Sister does as little as possible.'

'And if she can get out of the work altogether, she does!' Jessie added, darkly. 'I just wish Sister Ray would come back, but she's agreed to have the op, you know?'

'No, I didn't. I'm so glad!' Once she'd recovered from her hysterectomy Ros felt sure Sister Ray would be the same busy, brisk figure she remembered. 'She won't be back for months, then?'

Jessie shook her head. 'When I come back from leave it's possible they will ask me to act-up. I can see that you get all the experience you need, then.'

'Oh, Jessie, I hope you can! I can't take much more of that woman!' Or that man, Ros added but to herself. It wasn't Sister Rosebery who was the main problem!

There had, of course, been no opportunity to drop hints to Max Barrington about the nightclub, and Ros no longer cared, anyway. Even if he knew she was going he would not care, and she could hardly expect him to turn up at the club just to see Cinderella emerge from her pumpkin coach!

Ros was determined that she wouldn't go, Jessie equally determined that she should. And Jessie won, wearing Ros down by sheer persistence.

'And don't forget the new dress,' her friend said, firmly, after they had arranged the date. 'Something *special*.'

As it happened Ros had another invitation at about the same time—a telephone call from Danielle Dubois, inviting her to a housewarming party at her own home!

Ros couldn't believe her ears, and held the receiver away from her as if it was somehow to blame. *She* was being invited to a housewarming at Fairhaven! *She* was the hostess and ought to be doing the inviting, not the host's girlfriend!

'Miss Dubois,' Ros began firmly, 'It's very kind of you to invite me to a party but Fairhaven is *my* home, you know. Any invitations should come from the hostess.'

Danielle gasped. 'But I am the hostess!' she cried.

Ros could hear the rage in the other woman's voice. Do her good! 'I am part-owner of Fairhaven, Miss Dubois, and if there is a housewarming party to be arranged then it is up to Mr Barrington and myself to draw up a list of invitations.'

'But . . . No! This is impossible! I will not be treated this way!' Danielle exploded, her accent becoming thicker.

'As Mr Barrington is so busy I expect he's asked you to deal with the party for him,' Ros went on, beginning to enjoy herself. 'But I must be consulted as well. I want to see the guest-list.'

There was a stunned silence at the other end of the line and for a moment Ros thought Danielle was going to put the receiver down on her. 'I will speak to Max about this, Miss Hayward.' The honeyed sweetness was back in Danielle's tones. 'He particularly asked me to arrange a *man* for you,' Danielle went on. 'He said he felt sorry for you because you had no man of your own,' she continued, while Ros gripped the phone wire, tightly, wishing it was Max's throat. 'But if you take this attitude, I can do nothing for you! Nothing!'

The instrument clicked but Ros didn't put the receiver down straightaway, she was too stunned. Then anger brought her back to life. Mr Barrington needed taking down a peg or two!

It hurt. Even through her anger, Ros felt the knife

turning in her heart. He discussed her with his live-in girlfriend. They probably laughed about it. Max would tell Danielle amusing tales of how he had only to open his arms and poor little Rosalyn came running into them!

They jeered at her, despised her for enjoying his kisses, for wanting him to make love to her.

An anguished cry broke from her and she hurried up to the sanctuary of her room. If she was unhappy before, it was nothing compared with now. Her heart could hold no more sorrow, it was on the verge of shattering.

CHAPTER EIGHT

THE dress was black but there was nothing sombre about the material or the style. Black lace over a white silk shift. It was perfectly plain, as the saleslady had assured Ros that with her youth and English rose colouring she could get away with it. Could get away with murder might be more appropriate, she thought darkly, as she paraded in front of Jessie's critical eyes.

'Yes, it does something for you, Ros,' her friend agreed. 'I shouldn't have chosen black but it suits you. Gives you a tragic air,' she went on, thoughtfully.

That suited Ros' mood. She felt tragic after the set-to she'd had on the telephone with Danielle Dubois.

Two weeks had passed. Ros and Max had been icily polite to each other, though she had been careful to keep out of his way as much as possible, and she never ventured into the office unless absolutely necessary, in case Max should pay one of his unexpected visits. Visits that were becoming more frequent as he no doubt had plenty to discuss with his ex-girlfriend, Monica Rosebery.

On the last two occasions Ros had been busy at the opposite end of the ward, each time instructing a student nurse so Mr Barrington should have no cause to complain again. He hadn't torn her off a strip for upsetting Danielle, as she had half hoped he might. She was ready for him if he did!

Now it was the night of the housewarming. Ros had managed to wriggle out of going to the nightclub with

Jessie, pleading that she must save all her energy for the Fairhaven party. Danielle sent a list of all the people she and her fiancé wanted to invite, *had* invited, together with an ungracious little note informing Ros that if she wanted to invite anyone special they could cater only for another three or four.

Enraged, Ros felt like crossing off half the names on Danielle's list but would not resort to such spitefulness. If she was allowed four guests, then she would bring four. In the end it came to six, counting herself—Jessie and Brian, Everett Scott, and a person she thought of as a last resort, Barry Simpkin, her Aunt Gwen's solicitor. She asked him to bring a partner, so that made a nice round number.

Barry Simpkin had been in touch with Ros only once since he had taken her to Fairhaven. He was a somewhat pompous, fussy man, but basically kind and his dry sense of humour and funny little sayings made Ros laugh. They went some way towards making up for the nasty, vicious way the consultant treated her.

Given time she could get fond of Barry—they had graduated to first names by now. He wasn't exciting, nothing at all like the dark dynamic Max, and her heart didn't go bumpety-bump each time he came near, but it was just as well. Too much excitement might not be good!

Loving a man like Max, a girl would always either be in ecstasy, living on a cloud and polishing a fresh star every night, or else down in the slough of despond, wishing herself dead. All that up-and-down business couldn't be good for the system, Ros assured herself. Far better to be on the plateau all the time, with a nice, understanding man who made no demands, caused no excitement, but no anguish either.

But he was so old! Well, older than Max, she decided. He must be somewhere around forty if not more. Max was thirty-seven. Even thirty-seven was a lot, when one was only twenty-one and eleven-twelfths!

Still, I could keep him young! Ros told herself, as the chattering, friendly group made their way to Fairhaven in two cars. Everett had an old banger which didn't look all that roadworthy but Ros travelled with him, Barry Simpkin and Jessie following in Brian's Escort. Barry hadn't, after all, brought a partner but he didn't seem embarrassed at being the odd one out, especially when Ros assured him that the host's girlfriend had invited some Frenchwomen.

Fairhaven was ablaze with lights when they arrived. Ros had reluctantly relinquished her role as hostess to Danielle, who was undoubtedly more experienced at that sort of thing. Anyway, she did not appear to work for a living and had far more free time than Ros.

St Ann's seemed light years away as they entered the hall of Fairhaven, which was illuminated by a crystal chandelier Ros hadn't seen before.

Her lips tightened. Part of Mr Barrington's refurbishing? She had to admit it gave the cottage a certain air.

The perfect host was there to greet them, but there was no sign of the hostess. 'I am pleased you decided to come, Miss Hayward,' Max Barrington said, formally, shaking hands with her. It was more a touching of fingers than an actual handshake, but of course he had to be careful of his surgeon's fingers. Nevertheless, the brief touch set Ros aflame, and her eyes sparked fire at him.

'It *is* my home,' she said, with a quiet dignity her flashing eyes belied. 'Naturally I wanted to come to my *own* housewarming!'

Max gave her one of his famous haughty stares, but she didn't flinch. Then, with what she hoped was a merry sounding laugh she led her party towards the big sitting-room, Everett Scott hovering beside her, his hand just touching her elbow. Let Mr Barrington make two and two of that!

She shuddered when she saw that her Aunt's lovely furniture had been pushed back against the wall. She hoped none of it was damaged. The music was subdued and romantic, and Ros couldn't find fault with it. A stereo-player stood by the french windows, which were open to the balmy summer-night air. If it was possible to crowd another body into that space she would have been surprised. Ros didn't know any of the other guests and assumed they were Danielle's French friends.

Then she caught sight of Miss Merry, their PNO and she drew Jessie's attention.

'Well!' Jessie exclaimed. 'I thought she didn't like you-know-who. She does enjoy a good beano, so I expect she overcame her prejudices!'

'I know why she came!' Everett put in, dropping a boyishly friendly kiss on the top of Ros' elegant hair-do. 'She's cornered old Smith. She's fancied him for years!' He indicated the tall, thin man with whom Miss Merry was laughing.

I'm glad someone's happy, Ros thought wearily. She'd been on duty that day and should have finished at four-thirty. But Monica Rosebery made such a fuss about doing a split duty that Ros volunteered instead, so it was nearly eight before a vexed Everett Scott had managed to drag her away.

Of course Monica Rosebery didn't want to work late. She wanted plenty of time to get ready for the party. Ros and Jessie spotted her at the same moment—her bright auburn hair clashing with the flame-coloured dress she wore. Yet in a way it did not clash. It certainly made her stand out, and Ros admired her for having the courage to wear a colour like that. The dress had a three-tiered skirt and narrow shoulder straps. But Ros wanted to meet the surrogate hostess and had some difficulty in locating her.

Eventually they found Danielle in a quiet alcove, laughing up at a tall young man with a beard and dark glasses. Ros mentally shrugged. She didn't care for bearded men but evidently Danielle did.

They were speaking in French, a language Ros learned at school but hadn't bothered to keep up. She caught the odd word or two, though, and it didn't sound like a romantic conversation, more of a discussion about artists so perhaps bearded wonder was a famous French artist. Because their conversation wasn't intimate, Ros had no compunction about breaking into it.

'I was wondering where you were, Miss Dubois,' Ros began politely, and Danielle frowned.

'Oh, it is you! Excuse me,' she smiled up at her bearded friend then turned her attention to Ros and her friends. Evidently they were not good enough to be introduced to the Frenchman but Ros wasn't bothered. As long as Max saw that she was having a great time with Everett and Barry, Ros didn't care about any other men. She would *make* him notice her before the evening was out!

Danielle was polite to Ros' friends. Barry Simpkin, of course, she'd met before. Then with a confidential gesture she beckoned Ros closer, but raised her voice so that the others could hear: 'This man that Max insisted I find for you, there were not many to choose from,' Danielle said, clearly and slowly. 'But I have brought my

cousin, Jean-Pierre. He is unattached at the present.'
She shrugged, prettily. 'He is not much, you understand,
but all I could get for you. Poor Max *did* insist I found
you a man because you cannot find one of your own!' she
giggled, whilst Ros struggled to control her temper.

Everett and Barry went pink with embarrassment,
and Jessie and her fiancé stared, unable to believe the
Frenchwoman would be so blatantly rude.

'Please, Miss Dubois,' Ros said sweetly, 'there really
is no need to bother. As you and Mr Barrington can see I
have *two* young men so I don't need any left-over cousins
of yours!'

Danielle's hard mouth hardened still more, and her
pale eyes blazed at Ros.

Before there was an explosion, a cold foreign voice
broke in: 'As you say, Miss Hayward, you have plenty of
men for this evening. Perhaps another time Danielle can
find you a left-over cousin.'

Ros swung round, chilled to the marrow by the cold-
ness of Max's voice. Danielle laughed, a shrill chilly
sound, unmusical, screeching at her almost, and Ros felt
momentarily dizzy.

Max took hold of her forearm and swiftly led her to a
seat by the french windows. She sat, head bowed, then
felt warm hands on her neck as her head was forced
between her knees. She protested weakly that she was
fine but Max didn't let her up straight away.

Ros heard Jessie's voice as if from far off, then the
weakness and darkness receded, and she struggled
against the surgeon's restraining hand.

'You went white, Miss Hayward,' Max Barrington
informed her as he allowed her to sit up slowly. 'Perhaps
you have been drinking on an empty stomach?' he
suggested but Jessie cut in:

'We haven't been *offered* a drink yet, sir. More likely Staff Nurse Hayward is overtired. She was on duty until eight.'

He drew his heavy brows together, while Danielle gazed at the group, sulkily. 'I believed you to be on the early shift, Miss Hayward. Was this not so?'

Ros nodded, weakly. 'I stayed on a bit, sir.'

'Why?' he shot at her. 'Was there some trouble on the ward? Are you indispensable? Sister Rosebery was there. She couldn't get away any earlier and also came exhausted,' he carried on, accusingly.

Ros smiled bleakly at no-one in particular, and felt the gall rising within her. Blast Sister Rosebery! *She* had no reason to feel exhausted when it was Ros who had slaved away so the ward sister could get off early. It was no use telling old deep-freeze that, though, and she shook her head at Jessie when her friend seemed about to protest.

Ros got up, prepared to enjoy the party, *her* party, come what may, but instead of moving further into the room and joining the noisy throng, Max led her out onto the terrace and down the steps to the garden.

It was moonlight—a crescent moon suspended in a sky of midnight blue velvet—and Ros caught her breath at the wonder of it. It illuminated the garden sufficiently for them to see their way down a shorter flight of stone steps to the mini-orchard. Here there was silence except for the rustle of the trees in the warm breeze.

Ros had left her wrap indoors but was perfectly warm, more so when the tall, silent man by her side dropped his arm casually across her shoulders.

Max Barrington was sleek and suave in dinner jacket, his white shirt spartan in its plainness, she'd noticed before. He didn't speak, and she wondered, wistfully, if he had noticed her outfit. But why should he when once he'd seen Danielle he would have eyes for no other women, not even the flamboyantly-dressed Monica Rosebery. Danielle was in white, a flowing Grecian style that clung to her seductive curves. Diamonds flashed at her throat and ears. Gifts from the surgeon? No, he wasn't rich, only a consultant. However good their salary it did not put them in the millionaire class.

Danielle wore no rings except one plain ruby on her right hand, and Ros wondered where the engagement ring was. She supposed Danielle would choose a diamond, a solitaire probably. A big solitaire. Ros' own preference was for something smaller, a cluster of sapphires, perhaps. She smiled at the night, her heart crying within. Here she was strolling with another woman's lover! It was too poignant, too sad. She . . .

'I wish to talk to you, Rosalyn,' the surgeon said, gruffly, halting by the furthermost apple tree.

'Yes?' Ros' big eyes grew bigger and rounder as she tried to fathom out his expression in the dark. Was he about to officially announce his engagement, here at Fairhaven? She braced herself and waited.

'I think you should leave.'

'What?' At first she did not understand. 'Leave Fairhaven?' she asked, surprised.

'No, no! Ask to be moved from my wards!' Max snapped, gripping her by the wrists.

Numb with horror she could only stand quietly as his fingers probed the pulses at her wrists, pulses that were hammering away as she strove to absorb his remark. Then one hand moved sensuously up to the crook of her elbow where his thumb caressed the sensitive skin. Suddenly his arms were around her, and automatically she lifted her face for his kiss, a kiss of farewell.

His warm breath fanned her cheek, then his lips found

hers in a tender kiss, the faintest brush of mouth against mouth. Ros' lips parted in protest, and the kiss deepened, his tongue probing, seeking the honey, the sweetness within. She snuggled closer to him, unashamedly clinging because she knew this would be the last time he would take her in his arms. This was goodbye.

His hands moved caressingly over her body, her nipples rising to meet the demands of his hands. Her legs were rapidly turning to jelly, and somewhere a fire raged. She wanted this man, loved him, adored him. She longed to belong to him utterly. Yet it could never be.

Because at that moment she hated Danielle, the woman he had chosen, she pulled herself free, laughing hysterically.

'Rosalyn?' He spoke her name hesitantly, and the uncertainty in his voice broke her heart. He, who was always so sure, so definite.

She sobered, only the catch in her voice betraying the depth of her emotion. 'Please Mr Barrington . . . let's not get carried away. W . . . what will Danielle think?'

Ros raised her lovely eyes to his, hoping he would say he didn't care what Danielle thought, but he said nothing, merely gave a curiously foreign shrug.

'We had better go back,' Ros said huskily, cold now that she'd left the shelter of the surgeon's arms. She was more than cold, she was chilled to her very soul, and would never thaw again.

'Rosalyn,' he said again, and she turned, young and vulnerable, with the moonlight playing on her face.

He hesitated, then passed a hand wearily across his eyes. 'Nothing. It was nothing.' He led the way back towards the french windows, Ros following sadly.

The noise, the music and the talking reached a cres-

cendo as they approached, and Ros at that moment
hated them all.

No-one noticed their re-appearance, although it was
mere seconds before a dazzling Danielle glided towards
Max and tucked her arm in his. They spoke quietly in
French as they passed Ros, who went in search of a
drink. Any drink would do as long as it was strong!

A hand touched her lightly on the shoulder, and she
turned, knowing it would not be the one man for whom
she yearned. Barry Simpkin smiled at her, then offered
her the glass in his hand.

'Drink it up. You look ghastly!' he said, but his smile
was so tender that Ros couldn't take exception to his
remark.

She probably did look ghastly, she certainly felt it.
Her sad pansy-violet eyes followed Max and Danielle as
they mingled with their guests, then, raising her glass of
what looked like sherry, Ros proposed a toast to Barry's
continued good health 'and good business!' she added,
her soft kissable mouth curving into a smile.

It wasn't sherry, it was red Martini, and Ros drank it
quickly. Martini had an interesting effect on her, she'd
found out by accident one day, when as a teenager she
had raided her Aunt's cocktail cabinet. One Martini was
pleasant and gave her no trouble at all. Two Martinis
was even more pleasant and caused her a delicious sense
of well-being, of floating far above the clouds. When
Aunt Gwen found out she made Ros promise never to
drink more than one glass again.

It was a rule Ros had stuck to and seldom had the
opportunity of drinking anyway, but now she felt Aunt
Gwen would understand her need to feel lighter than air,
so she didn't feel guilty when she asked Barry to get her a
refill.

His shrewd eyes seemed to reproach her, but he did as he was asked and came back with a Martini for Ros and a beer for himself. 'Here, drink and be merry for tomorrow we die!' he quipped. 'Or did you die tonight?'

'I beg your pardon?' Ros, face flushed, wouldn't meet his gaze. She tried to laugh off the question. 'I don't *think* I've died yet. Can't hear any angel choirs!'

'Don't be facetious, Ros,' Barry said, sternly. 'I had the feeling that, well, that you rather fancied that foreign fellow.'

'F . . . foreign fellow? Which one?' Ros' eyes were wide and luminous, and bright with unshed tears.

Gently the solicitor removed her half-empty glass. Inwardly shrugging, she let him take it away.

'The food's nearly all gone. They didn't make a very sound job of catering, did they?' Barry led her away, talking of inconsequential matters, and silently Ros thanked him.

He was rather bossy, a bit prim and proper, but oh, how kind he was! And kindness was something of which Ros was sorely in need.

Several times during the evening she caught sight of Danielle or Max, but they were never together. Danielle kept with her French friends. One of them she brought over to Ros and Barry.

Ros eyed him, doubtfully. This must be the cousin Danielle had imported in her honour. He was of medium height, with dark hair and eyes. Nothing spectacular about him, except for those eyes. They were peculiarly Gallic. They had a luminosity, a deepness, a life of their own, and Ros found him charming. Too charming, perhaps, as he laid on the compliments with a house-painter's brush, but it made a pleasant interlude, and

Barry, though stiff with him at first, was gradually melted by Jean-Pierre's charm.

But it was Barry who invited her out. Several of the guests had gone, the party had quietened, and Ros was reflectively chewing a peanut when Barry hesitantly asked if he might see her again.

Startled, Ros turned her lovely eyes on him. 'Why of course you can see me again! I'm always there—at St Ann's I mean. Or here. Heavens! It's my holiday next week!' So much had happened that her approaching leave had slipped into the background. 'Two weeks of heaven. And I can spend it here!' she beamed. 'At least I hope I can.' Her eyes saddened. What a fool she was to be happy, excited. Fairhaven seemed no longer her home.

'It's full of strangers,' she said, disconsolately. 'Fairhaven—I wanted to spend my holiday here but maybe Mr Barrington had other plans . . .'

'Then he must change them!' the solicitor said, briskly. He squeezed her arm. 'I'll go and settle it with him. When does your holiday start?'

'On Monday, but . . .' She had no chance to tell Barry she didn't want him to settle it with the surgeon. It was something for her and her co-owner to sort out between them.

She watched, without appearing to, as the two men talked. Once, the surgeon glanced over at her, and Ros could feel the intensity of that gaze but pretended not to see. Then Barry moved away and to Ros' horror, Max made purposefully for her.

Nervously she watched him approach. She was rooted to the spot, and even if he had been a charging bull elephant she doubted if she could have moved.

She might be *safer* with a bull elephant, she thought,

seeing with dismayed eyes the tight, glowering expression on his face. One charge and it would all be over.

'Am I to understand that you are on leave next week, Miss Hayward?' Max asked tightly, and Ros nodded, a tendril of hair escaping from the sophisticated chignon.

'You look absurdly young like that,' he went on, his black eyes sliding over her.

She opened her mouth, then ran her tongue nervously over her lips. 'I . . . I'm not *that* young!' she protested, but very weakly. 'Yes, I shall be on two weeks' leave— from Monday,' she hurried on, as those disturbing eyes rested on her mouth. Her lipstick hadn't the staying power of her usual brand and she felt certain she looked a mess. Certainly her nose must be shiny by now, and Jessie had pointed out that Ros had the beginnings of a ladder in her sexy sheer black tights.

Sadly she gazed at the object of her dreams and waited for him to make some disparaging comment.

'Why did you not tell me yourself?' he enquired, instead, his voice husky, seductive. He moved nearer, bending his head so that she was compelled to meet that enticing, exciting gaze. Her view of the room was blocked off by his head and they might have been the only people in the world. She closed her eyes, the intensity of her emotion momentarily too much for her.

Gently his finger touched her eyelids, and her eyes sprang open. 'I . . . I'm sorry. I expect I'm tired.' She excused her lapse, with a deprecating little laugh.

'You should not close them. You have beautiful eyes—the colour of a stormy sky when the thunderheads build up. Then lightning flashes and the violet sky turns dark and sombre. But you must never be that, Rosalyn,' he went on, seductively.

Like a frightened gazelle she was rooted to the spot,

while the hunter edged nearer. 'That dress. I do not like it. Such colours are for older ladies.'

'Yes? I mean, are they? I thought black suited me,' she hurried on, finding her voice. Not that she intended arguing with him. Oh, no. Anything but argument!

'No! You will wear white in future!' he insisted, and faint colour tinged her cheeks.

Virginal white. He was treating her like a schoolgirl! What made him think she was so young and untouched anyway? He had a nerve, when it was obvious he preferred his women experienced!

Let him believe she *was* experienced! Then perhaps he would become interested. By the time he realised his mistake he might not mind her innocence, might be prepared to teach her all she needed to know about pleasing men. About pleasing *him*, she corrected herself, sternly. The idea brought a fresh blush, and Max eyed her, his brows raised.

'My suggesting you wear white embarrasses you, Rosalyn? How can this be? Such innocence, such loveliness as yours should not be hidden beneath a dark colour.'

Ros grew redder, though more with anger now. He needn't keep on about her innocence. He must think her very naive. Well, she would show him! She lowered her eyes, then peeked at him through long, gold-tipped lashes. 'Perhaps *white* is not the ideal colour for me, Mr Barrington,' she said, sweetly. 'After all, this isn't the East, you know. English girls don't go around chaperoned or walk about in long black cloaks!'

He frowned, then his handsome face resumed its usual impassive haughty expression. 'True. Forgive me for sullying your reputation, Rosalyn.' He gave a mocking half-bow then strolled away, tall, dark and hateful!

Ros almost choked, she was so angry. But at least she'd made her point, and his interest might have been aroused.

Her sad eyes lit up as Barry made his way towards her. 'Your friends are ready to go now, Ros. Did you settle everything? Dates, times of vacating?'

'What?'

'With Mr Barrington,' he said, patiently. 'Did you tell him when you want to move in?'

'Oh, that. Yes, I said I began my holiday on Monday, but . . .' She had forgotten what she was supposed to discuss with the surgeon. Now, her eyes sought him. He was nowhere to be seen, but Danielle's distinctive seductive laugh came from somewhere, and Ros, miserable and ill at ease, almost dragged Barry Simpkin through the door. She had to get away. Hopefully Fairhaven would be cleaned up again by Monday but if not she could do it herself. The consultant might want to be here for the weekends so she would return to St Ann's on Friday night leaving the cottage for him. He might well want Danielle there for the weekend. The thought of them together was almost more than Ros could bear, but she would survive.

Dear, kind Barry would help her. She smiled up at him, and gently he patted her hand. Yes, he would take care of her. She didn't *need* the Max Barringtons of this world.

CHAPTER NINE

Ros floated lazily, her eyes closed against the glare of the sun. This was heaven! The heatwave held for her holiday, at least it had done so far, and she'd been completely alone except for her transistor and her record-player, both of which she had transported from St Ann's.

Reluctantly, she got out of the pool, water glistening on her fair skin. The black and white bikini was just a shade too big. She untied the ill-fitting top. She was alone and the swimming pool could not be seen from the road. She could, in any case, hear a car approaching if she sat just outside the french windows.

She dried her feet, slipped into espadrilles, then wandered contentedly into the kitchen. A long, cool drink would be the perfect end to her swim. She . . .

'Enjoyed your swim?'

'Erk!' The hand she intended should open the fridge door went instead to cover her bare breasts, as the hateful surgeon smiled at her.

He was straddling the old kitchen chair, tie loosened, a lazy grin on his hard face, his eyes on her body.

'I . . . excuse me!' She ran out, back to the pool to retrieve her bikini-top, then stood for a moment to recover. It was just like him to creep up on her! The nerve of the man!

Not content with replacing the bikini-top, she added a long, brightly-coloured towelling robe for good measure, then walked reluctantly back to the kitchen.

Max was still where she'd left him. 'Why cover your-self? I have seen women's breasts before. Yours are nothing special,' he added unkindly, and Ros wanted to strike him.

Instead, she said icily: 'May I ask what you want, Mr Barrington?'

He grinned, his dark eyes mocking her, and she went scarlet.

'Oh, you blush again. Can it be that you are *not* the experienced lover you assured me you were?'

'I never . . . ! I mean, I didn't tell you anything about my past!' she flared, then remembered the one and a half Martinis she'd drunk at the party. Had she said some-thing unwise? She wrinkled her brow in thought, then ran a hand distractedly through her hair, which hung loose and wet to her shoulders. 'I can't remember,' she admitted.

'So? Let me refresh your memory. You told me at the party that white was not your colour. You excite me, Rosalyn.' With the suddenness of a panther he sprang. One moment he was astride the chair several feet away, the next he was standing beside her frightened, trem-bling body. 'You are not very efficient as a nurse, but as a woman I believe you will be satisfactory.'

He almost drawled the word 'satisfactory' and Ros shook with anger. 'I don't *want* to be satisfactory!' she flared, fighting off his hands. Heavens, the man must be an octopus!

He had, it seemed, only two hands after all, and two very strong arms which held her easily against his chest. 'Why must you fight me? Surely I am not unattractive?' he said, with his lips against her ear, and she struggled the harder. 'Perhaps I have not the technique of the red-faced one? Is that it?'

'Red-faced one?' She stopped her struggles, her gaze surprised.

'The lawyer. He has a red face, also, he is losing his hair. But, see, I have plenty.' Max took her hand and eased it through his thick, glossy mane of black hair.

She gave a little moan, then went on running her fingers through its crispness without further help. He was right, Barry's hair *was* thinning.

'He's very kind to me,' Ros said, snatching her hand away from his hair. 'Barry, I mean. He cares about me!'

'Ah, yes, he cares, but for what?' the surgeon said, smugly. 'It may be that it is Fairhaven for which he is caring so much, not you.'

'No! You shouldn't say things like that!' she protested, eyes anguished. Of course Barry cared for her. He wasn't after the cottage. Why should he be? He must have a detached house of his own somewhere.

Ros found that her head was resting against the surgeon's chest now, and it felt good. It felt so right— almost as if she belonged there. But he was interested in only one thing. He didn't want Ros, he wanted her body. Hadn't he said as much?

Satisfactory! He had no right. She opened her pretty mouth to tell him so, but that was a mistake. His mouth swooped down on hers, and she saw stars, heard sweet voices singing. His teeth ground against hers, his tongue probing and seeking, and the sweet voices stopped singing. He was going to rape her! They were alone in this isolated house. There was no escape!

Terrified, she fought him but his arms tightened. Ros moaned when he gave her a fleeting chance to breathe, then almost collapsed against him, all thoughts of escape flying out of her mind, as her legs turned to jelly. Her senses demanded this man. Whatever his own reasons, hers were quite clear—she loved him and that was all that mattered.

Rough hands tore the robe from her shoulders then, in moments, the irksome bikini-top joined it on the floor. She quivered, hoping he would be gentle yet doubting it.

But he was; before she was fully aware of what was happening, she was swung up into his arms and carried through to the sitting-room, the scene of last Friday's party.

Gently he lowered her onto the soft, plush settee, then one hand closed possessively over her small firm breast and she shuddered, desire running through her slender frame.

At some point he must have discarded his shirt, for his chest was warm and bare against hers, the hair tickling her breasts. His body was hard and heavy on hers, then she tensed as his hand moved lazily across her stomach, then onto her thigh.

For a few seconds she couldn't move, had no power to prevent what he was doing, but the waves of desire receded as she became aware of her nakedness. Horrified and ashamed, bitterly ashamed, she thrust aside his probing hands, and tried to leap from the settee but landed in an ungainly quivering heap on the thick carpet.

She hid her crimson face in the carpet as she lay prone, shielding her naked body from his gaze. A sob broke from her, then another, her slight frame racked with them. They were tears of shame as well as sorrow. Never, never should she have allowed such liberties!

Realisation of how much of her she'd allowed him to fondle and kiss revolted her. How he must be laughing now! Gradually her crying ceased, and the room grew quiet. Cold now, she sat up and reached for the discarded towelling robe which was in a neat pile by her feet, together with her bikini.

Clutching the robe to her breasts, she turned sad, wondering eyes on the surgeon who, now fully clothed, looked down at her from his great height.

'You should not have tempted me, Rosalyn,' he said, sombrely. 'I believed you innocent, yet you suggested otherwise.'

Ashamed, Ros cast her eyes down. It was true. She had wanted him to believe her experienced, so was it his fault that he had?

'You have a beautiful body,' he went on, slowly. 'Young and firm and supple. I envy the man to whom you will give yourself one day.' There was a deep sadness in his voice which touched a raw nerve, and Ros met his gaze, her eyes a deep violet in her anguish.

'For when you give your body you will also give your heart,' the surgeon said, gently, and Ros nodded, knowing it to be true. 'I almost wish I could be that fortunate man.' Max's wide mouth smiled but his eyes remained sad, and Ros wanted to fling herself into his arms, comfort and hold him, tell him that he *was* the man of whom he spoke.

She almost did, but before she could speak, Max shook his head as if to clear it. 'But I am not that man,' he said, heavily. 'Come, replace your clothes which I have brought in, then you can go and wash your face. I need a drink.' He strode from the room and her eyes smarted with unshed tears.

She loved him! She must tell him, assure him that it was in love she had offered herself. She *must* tell him!

Quickly, she pulled the bikini on, then, carrying the robe, she went in search of him. He was in the study which overlooked the small front garden. Music from her own record-player provided a soft, muted background as, with love in her eyes, she approached.

'Aha! Scotch. This is what I need!' the surgeon joked, then tipped back his head and took a long drink from the bottle. A little wary, Ros stepped back, aware from her A & E days of what the demon drink could do to otherwise pleasant people.

'Please,' she began, staying well out of his reach, 'there's something I *must* tell you!'

'So?' He put down the bottle then frowned at it, while Ros waited impatiently to regain his attention. 'Danielle, she is waving, jewellers catalogues at me,' he said reflectively, and Ros' heart tumbled to her bare feet.

'She insists on the biggest diamond I can afford! Perhaps she should marry a diamond-mine millionaire!' He laughed harshly, his eyes cold and empty now as they rested on Ros' crestfallen face. Then he shrugged. 'She will be a good mother to Anne-Marie. They understand each other, I think. It is for my daughter's happiness I am concerned,' he went on, half to himself, while Ros listened numbly.

'Yes? You wanted to tell me something of great importance?' The surgeon seemed to jerk himself back from the unhappy past, remembering that Ros wanted to speak to him.

She shook her head, trying to form her lips into a smile but making a poor job of it. 'No,' she whispered, 'it wasn't at all important.'

Sadly she wandered off, her numb legs carrying her up to the bathroom. She stripped off, throwing the hated bikini into a corner. Never again would she wear it. After a hasty shower, she washed her face as instructed then went in search of fresh clothing. She padded about naked, but knew she was perfectly safe. The surgeon, now assured of her inexperience, would not touch her again. With Max Barrington she was safe.

That she did not want to be safe was of no consequence. And, in a way, it was comforting. With a sad smile on her small face, Ros, now casually dressed in plain white blouse and paisley skirt, went to find the surgeon. She must ask him what he was doing here when he should have been in the operating theatre. Had something happened at St Ann's?

She found him sitting by the pool, a glass and the whisky bottle near to hand. He'd shed the jacket of his lightweight suit, his shirt was unbuttoned to the waist, and he wore sun-glasses, just like any tourist.

Hesitantly, Ros approached and he patted the chair beside him. 'Here, come and sit. We must talk.'

Ros sat down at his bidding, her bare legs crossed primly at the ankles. They both spoke together, but the surgeon indicated that she should continue. 'I only wanted to ask—why you're here, I mean. Shouldn't you be in theatre?' Ros asked shyly, almost calling him 'sir' but remembering in time. After their recent closeness she couldn't call him that!

'I should be, but du Carle wanted tomorrow off. Had some meeting I believe, so tomorrow I will take my list. He is operating today.'

'Oh, I see.' St Ann's had inadequate theatre accommodation and this sometimes happened. They needed more space. All St Ann's shortcomings rushed to meet her and she wondered anew why a man such as Max Barrington should leave his previous well-equipped hospital to work there. When she asked, he seemed surprised.

'Is it not obvious, then?'

Her eyes darkened with sadness. He was confirming

the rumour that he'd followed Monica Rosebery to Suffolk. Or was it Fairhaven that drew him eastward?

'Your home. I mean where you're living now. Is it very big? Like Fairhaven, I mean?'

'It is a rented cottage. Quite small by Fairhaven standards, but very pretty. Anne-Marie likes living there but sometimes she is lonely.'

'An only child often is,' Ros put in.

'But, who knows? Anne-Marie may not always be an only one. I should like a son.'

'Oh, yes. Yes, I suppose you would,' Ros said, forlornly, trying to picture Danielle crooning to a small, newly-born Max Barrington Junior, and failing utterly. The woman wasn't motherly! He was making a mistake marrying her, but Ros could hardly tell him so. He would consider Ros herself far too young, too immature, to be a mother. Particularly to Anne-Marie, who was nearly seven. Ros' heart ached for Max and for the little girl when Danielle joined their family, but it wasn't any of her business.

'I wish to speak of the unfortunate incident,' Max said suddenly, and Ros began to interrupt, to assure him she didn't want him to mention it again. The whole embarrassing, disgusting episode was better forgotten.

He raised a hand for silence and Ros automatically obeyed.

'Listen to me, then we will not speak of it again,' he began. 'Now that I am assured of your innocence I wish to protect you, be the father of which you are sorely in need.'

'But . . .' she began, then was irritably waved to silence again.

'I know. My behaviour was anything but fatherly!' Max admitted, with a wry smile. 'But in the future I assure you I will behave as a father ought. Look upon me as your protector, Rosalyn. I should like that very much.' He held out his hand in a gesture of friendship and hesitantly Ros put her small slim hand in his large one.

He squeezed her fingers gently, then released her hand. 'Good. We are friends then?'

She nodded. 'Friends.' She couldn't see his eyes, could not gauge his feelings because of the dark glasses he wore, but she thought his eyes smiled at her for once.

Friends. Better that than nothing. She needed a friend, someone strong on whom to lean occasionally, but she had never visualised the consultant in that role!

'One day you will marry,' he went on, idly. 'But you must be sure. I beg of you not to marry just *any* man. He must be someone special, someone set apart,' he urged.

Without thinking, Ros said: 'He is. Special, I mean.' Then she looked away, biting her lip miserably. She'd nearly told him. Would he suspect?

It seemed he did not because he frowned, ominously. 'This man. Is it the lawyer? He is not for you!' he said decisively, and Ros looked up in astonishment at the vehemence in his tone.

'Why not? He would take care of me, protect me.'

'Yes, that is true, but he is too old, too set in his ways.'

'No, he is not!' Ros cried. 'You've seen his sportscar. That isn't the sort of car a fuddy-duddy drives!'

'Fuddy-duddy.' He tried the expression and it sounded so strange coming from him that Ros smiled, impishly.

'It means someone set in his ways, as you implied Barry was. He's kind. He wouldn't ever hurt me,' she went on, knowing it to be true.

'He is not suitable for you,' Max declared. 'I will try to find you someone younger.'

'No! I will not have you husband-hunting for me!' she said, indignantly. 'What about Jean-Pierre? I was embarrassed when Miss Dubois said you asked her to find me a man! It was awful!'

'I said no such thing!' he thundered, his face darkening with anger. 'I requested that she find you a partner for the evening. No more. Did her cousin misbehave?'

'Oh, no. He was quite nice. Very charming,' Ros assured him, pleased that it hadn't been as Danielle suggested. He hadn't told Danielle that Ros couldn't get a man of her own, she was sure of that now. It was Danielle being bitchy.

'There's Everett Scott,' she suggested, wondering what his reaction would be.

'No! I will not permit that!' he snapped.

Ros' eyes widened. 'There's no need to sound so violent! Everett is quite a nice boy. And he isn't that much older,' she pointed out, wondering what he disliked about the big registrar.

'He is not suitable,' Max said, stubbornly, then dropped the subject and went on to talk about his childhood in Hungary.

Ros followed his lead and they discussed safe topics for a while, then he glanced at his watch and flicked her a lazy grin. 'I think you should prepare my lunch now,' he laughed.

Ros shook her fist at him, but obeyed willingly. She would wait on him hand and foot if that would please him. She would do anything just to have him smile regularly at her!

After lunch, a simple salad accompanied by slices of cold beef, they relaxed on the terrace. Ros lay back on the chaise longue which Max had dragged out for her, a contented smile on her lips. Nearby, Max sat on the top step, smoking a cheroot, the pleasant, pungent aroma tickling her nostrils. It was the first time she'd seen him smoke and he told her he did so only at home, after his evening meal. Then he enjoyed a cheroot and a glass of whisky and soda, or perhaps a liqueur.

It pleased her that he felt at home here, with her. They could be any contented married couple, gazing out happily at their domain. Except that they were not married, and he was engaged to someone else.

Love shouldn't make people feel older but it did. Ros felt she'd aged ten years since she'd known Max Barrington. She felt old enough, mature enough, to cope with this difficult, prickly man and his daughter. But she couldn't tell him and there was no way he would find out otherwise.

She gazed at the back of his head, at the black hair worn rather long, at his powerful shoulders and broad back tapering to narrow hips. She loved every inch of him and wanted to care for him, in sickness as well as in health. Why couldn't he see she loved him? Why?

The day passed delightfully after that. They strolled side by side but not touching, down through the orchard where he had kissed her in the moonlight only a few nights previously. Later, after a snack tea, they lazed by the poolside, enjoying the inactivity. For both of them work was a hard grind, a ceaseless scurrying about for her, and for him an endless round of decisions to be made, lives to be saved. It was good to have this time together, to pretend they were rich and didn't need to work. For Ros it was bitter-sweet, knowing this might be the last day they spent together. So, just for a while, she pretended that there was no tomorrow, only today.

Glancing back at Fairhaven, her legacy, she saw it as a legacy of love. For love had created it, Aunt Gwen's love for the old cottage had made it what it was. And she and Max together would improve and renovate it, so that it always remained a legacy of love.

Would he and Danielle want to live there? she wondered not for the first time. If his present cottage was small, naturally he must move.

She could not bear to have Danielle live at Fairhaven, but if it was what Max wanted she would agree. She wouldn't ask yet. Reluctant to break the enchanted spell, she didn't want to talk at all.

Max did not, as she half-hoped, invite her to dine out. As evening bore down on them, the shadows lengthened and a cool breeze began to blow.

Ros shivered, knowing she must move yet wanting to savour every moment. He wasn't going to invite her out to dinner. That much was obvious, as he yawned and stretched, murmuring lazily that he ought to move.

She caught the name 'Danielle' and her heart lurched, sickeningly. Always Danielle.

'Where is Anne-Marie today? Isn't Miss Dubois looking after her?'

'No, I cannot take advantage of Danielle's kindness to that extent,' he said, and Ros wondered idly what exactly he did expect of Danielle. 'Anne-Marie is with a group of school-friends. They are at some camp for the day. A nature trail, I believe it is called.'

'Anne-Marie will like that.'

'No, she will not!' he put in, sourly. 'You must have seen that she is a feminine little girl, all frills and flounces and jewels. She did not want to go. There will be boys there, she said! She takes after her mother, does not care to dirty her hands.'

'Oh! She . . . does she look like her mother?' Ros asked, tentatively, wondering if Anne-Marie was the sweet-natured doll she appeared to be.

'Mm. She gets her colouring from Marguerite. Also from my grandmother who was fair. By rights she should be dark of eye and dark of hair. Something must have gone wrong with Mendel's peas!' he joked.

'Mendel's peas? Oh, you mean the Mendelian Law?'

He nodded. 'Dominant genes. Because dark is dominant and fair is recessive, Anne-Marie should have black hair and eyes, like myself. Instead she inherited fair genes from her mother and, of course, from my grandmother. Poor Abbe Mendel would be put out!'

'She's pretty, though. If she *did* have black eyes, she would be stunning,' Ros said reflectively, and he grunted his agreement.

'It is cold now and you must put on more clothes,' he ordered, getting up and folding away his chair. 'I want you full of life when you return to St Ann's.'

'So that you can shout at me?' she put in, peeved because he seemed eager to leave, to go home to Danielle.

He stared down at her, eyes narrowed. She thought he might kiss her, or make a joke about shouting at her but he did not. 'All I *can* do is shout at you, Rosalyn,' he said, quietly.

After Max had gone Ros wandered slowly about, touching items he had touched, the chaise longue, his deck-chair, a glass, trying to recapture his presence, trying to keep a little of the precious magic for herself. Her head and her heart ached. In fact her whole body ached. She wanted Max, loved him, yet he must love Danielle, surely? He was in a hurry to return home. Had said as much.

No tears came, and she lay awake for much of the night dry-eyed and sick at heart. She couldn't cry. The time for tears, healing, cleansing tears, was past. She must be strong, put this hopeless love to one side, concentrate on being what she knew would make Max happy—an efficient, conscientious staff nurse.

The remainder of her holiday dragged. Max had told her that while she was on holiday he would not interrupt it, that she could spend the two weekends at Fairhaven as well.

Jessie was off all day Saturday as Sister Rosebery wanted Sunday and Monday for some reason. She spent the day at Fairhaven and that helped pass the time. Twice during the second week Barry Simpkin called and they spent the whole of Ros' last day, a Sunday, together. They couldn't sit out because it rained almost the whole day, so Ros showed him over Fairhaven, which he hadn't seen in its entirety. When, face glowing, she told him of the improvements Max was hoping to make, Barry pursed his lips.

'It will be a great expense, Ros. He will expect you to pay half, you know,' he warned, but Ros assured him that the surgeon would foot the bill.

'He said all I had to pay for was my food. Isn't that kind?' she enthused, then her concerned gaze caught the doubting expression in his grey eyes before he once again became the expressionless man of law.

'*Don't* you think it's kind of him?' Ros persisted. They were in the small, homely study, and the staccato beat of raindrops upon the window was a chorus that seemed to echo her words.

Barry rubbed the back of his head, reflectively. 'It

depends. On his reasons for taking on the financial burden, I mean.' He hesitated, shrewd eyes assessing her probable reaction. 'Could it be that he has designs on the complete cottage? On the *whole* of Fairhaven?'

Ros wanted to jump up in protest, but there could be a germ of truth in what the solicitor suggested, though Max himself had said the same thing about Barry!

'You obviously had the same thought,' Barry was saying, and Ros cast him a worried look.

'He can't, can he? Get control of Fairhaven, I mean?'

'It was left to you fifty-fifty so he can't sell it over your head, no. But you ought to be paying half the expenses. Have you anything in writing?'

'In writing? About him agreeing to renovate and improve Fairhaven?'

'Yes. Always have it in writing,' Barry urged. 'I know I sound like an old fuddy-duddy,' he went on, and Ros giggled, remembering her conversation with Max. 'I'm doing it for you, Ros,' he urged. 'Let me deal with the business side of it for you. Keep the sharks at bay.'

'Mr Barrington is *not* a shark!' Ros spoke more sharply than she'd intended, and her guest reddened.

'Oh, please! I didn't mean to snap at you! You've been so kind.' Poor Ros was more distressed than Barry.

Gently, he trailed a finger down her slender cheek, stopping at her mouth. Her lips parted uncertainly, and he kissed them, a faint brushing of mouth against mouth, the way Max sometimes did.

No bells rang, no cymbals clashed, and Ros felt sadder than ever. Barry tried so hard, he deserved better.

'I'm sorry,' he said, his large, protruding eyes sad. 'I tried not to but I'm afraid I've fallen in love with you, Ros.'

Ros opened her mouth, then closed it again. What

could she say? 'I . . .' she tried again. 'Oh, Barry!' I had no idea! I mean, I'm not at all lovable.'

'But you are! You're everything I've ever dreamed of,' he assured her, drawing her close. He spread his large hands about her slender waist, and squeezed gently.

When, in her numbed state, she didn't protest, he held her more tightly and bent his head to kiss her. Then she did come to life. 'Please, Barry! You're hurting!'

Indeed, he was, his hands leaving a red mark on her bare arms.

'Ros! I'm sorry!' Tenderly, he stroked her arms, trying to erase the marks he had made.

Ros stood patiently, not feeling the thrill, the desire that Max's touch brought. And Max, for all his temper, never marked her. It was only her heart he bruised.

'Ros! My dear, speak to me!' Barry shook her, drawing her out of the brown study into which she'd sunk. Everything came back to Max. If only she'd never met him!

'I'm fine now,' she assured Barry, a sad smile touching her lips. 'Perhaps you should go. It's getting late.'

Darkness was falling and it was a long way for him to drive. In the dark, the narrow twisty lanes could be treacherous. And they would be wet and sticky with the day's rain.

He laughed shortly. 'Hardly the night for driving, is it? Would . . . would you mind my staying here? I could sleep in Anne-Marie's bed. Or on the settee,' he suggested, and Ros didn't know how to refuse him.

If he left and met with an accident, she would never forgive herself. She didn't want him to stay but would not hurt his feelings by telling him, so nodded her acquiescence.

'I'll make you up a bed. You can use the master bedroom.' Quickly she prepared the bed for Barry, feeling that the sooner he got to bed the sooner morning would come and he could leave!

The master bedroom was where Max slept when he visited at weekends. He'd told her that, otherwise she would not have known because there was no visible sign of his presence, no hairbrushes, clothing, toilet articles, nothing at all to indicate that Max slept there. He even brought his own bed-linen or else he used a sleeping-bag! There was no outward sign of Danielle's presence, either. They must both travel light. Not even a bottle of perfume showed that Danielle spent weekends there.

Anne-Marie's bedroom was used, that much was obvious, and Ros made a point of going in there just to touch the girl's few possessions. By so doing she could conjure up a picture of Anne-Marie's father. It was little enough.

After an early supper, eaten in a strained silence, they went to bed. Ros, without understanding why, locked her bedroom door. It wasn't that she didn't trust Barry exactly, but there was no point in taking chances.

Ros was on early next day, and was glad of a lift from Barry. He helped her with her suitcase and various parcels, even carrying them up to her room for her.

They parted amicably, Barry promising to take her to a concert in Cambridge a few days later. He was kind, Ros reflected, and he would take care of her. She couldn't have Max so why not Barry? Why not take what he offered?

She wasn't a girl to settle for second-best, but . . .

'Hi! Penny for them?' Jessie bounded into the lift going up to Women's Surgical.

'I was rearranging my life,' Ros remarked. 'Surely we aren't both on early?'

'Sister Rosebery is back on Men's Surgical,' Jessie told her. 'So from today I am acting Sister Bradley. You will treat me with the contempt my position warrants!' she quipped, and Ros, feeling lighter at heart than she'd done for weeks, hurried into the staff room to shed her cloak.

No Sister Rosebery! It was too good to be true. No Max Barrington, either, until this afternoon when he was due to do a quick round, seeing only selected patients.

'Should have been here this morning,' Jessie explained, 'but he's put it back till two o'clock. I think he's taking the girl-friend out to buy the ring this morning. Perhaps I got hold of the wrong end of the stick though. Might have.' Jessie sorted out the work-book, but Ros was only half-aware of what the staff nurse was telling her.

Taking the girl-friend to buy the ring. It wasn't plausible. He would not leave his patients just to take Danielle out. It wasn't his way. Yet there might be something in it. It could be today that Danielle would be choosing her ring. Diamonds, Max told her. Danielle wanted a big, big diamond.

'Have you heard a word I've said?' The usually sunny-natured Jessie actually snapped, and Ros started, guiltily.

'I'm all ears, really, Jessie. I just missed the last bit.'

Jessie shot her a sharp look. 'He's heavily engaged elsewhere, Ros. He's way out of your league.'

'Is it that obvious?' Ros asked miserably, and her friend nodded. 'I'm very sorry, Jessie.'

'I hope you are. Far better to settle for someone in

your own firmament rather than setting your cap at another universe. There's always Everett Scott. Anyway, to work,' Jessie went on, briskly, and Ros threw herself into the ward-work, leaving herself no time to think, to daydream.

As two p.m. approached though, Ros became on edge. She went to late lunch but was back by one-thirty to help prepare the patients for Max's round.

At exactly two o'clock the doors swung open and Max and his retinue approached. Jessie, of course, took the round, with a third-year student wheeling the Kardex. Ros' job was to answer the telephone, deal with any emergencies and generally supervise the ward while Jessie was involved with the surgeons.

Max didn't appear to notice Ros and she didn't push herself forward. With any luck she need not see him at all. She could find work in the ward itself while he wrote up his notes in the office.

Unfortunately, once the round was complete and the party were heading for the ward-office, the telephone rang and Ros couldn't escape in time. It was only a routine call from Admin, but by the time she'd finished the dark, brooding presence of Max Barrington was beside her, his eyes resting on her speculatively, as if believing it was a private call.

They exchanged a polite 'good-afternoon' then, with a sigh of relief, Ros hurried back to the ward. She heard the phone ring again but Jessie would answer it now.

'Mrs Clift, Staff. Will you supervise her dressing?' It was the new second-year Avril Paige, Leonora having finished her stint on Jevington.

Ros was about to oblige when, out of the corner of her eye, she saw Mr Barrington beckoning from the office window. Surely she couldn't be needed. After all, she had been off for two weeks and hadn't had a chance to read all the case-notes though she'd done her best.

With a feeling of impending doom, Ros hurried to the office.

CHAPTER TEN

MAX Barrington stood by the door to Jessie's office, face like thunder, and Ros skidded to a halt in front of him.

'I have told you before that the ward telephone is for ward use only,' he began, each word dripping with ice, and Ros felt sick inside. Who could possibly have phoned her?

'It was your . . . *friend* on the telephone, Staff Nurse!' Max snapped. 'Mr Simpkin, the solicitor. Said to thank you for your hospitality last night—*all* night.'

Ros put a hand up to her burning cheek. This was all she needed!

'He went on to tell me that the bed was most comfortable—and warm,' the consultant went on, disgust in his voice, which he kept low. 'Why was it warm, Miss Hayward? An old-fashioned bed-warmer, perhaps? An electric blanket? Or did *you* warm him up yourself!' he hissed, face only inches from her own.

'But I didn't!' Ros protested, trying to keep her voice to a whisper. 'He asked and I didn't like to refuse,' she assured him, but he must have misunderstood.

'I hope he appreciated what you gave him, Miss Hayward!' he whispered fiercely, then brushed past her, followed after a decent interval by Everett, who raised his eyebrows at her as he passed.

Ros wanted to die. And Jessie's astonished gaze made it clear that she had heard part, at least, of the exchange.

Jessie understood after Ros explained, but it was clear that the surgeon believed the worst.

'He wants to believe the worst!' Ros exploded, nearly in tears. 'He hates me!'

'No, he doesn't, Ros. You're being childish!' Jessie said, firmly. 'He thinks none of us are as good as his London nurses and that's that. Nothing will make him change his opinion.'

'It's me he has his knife into,' Ros insisted, stubbornly. 'If only you knew!'

On Tuesday Max Barrington walked into the ward-office as Ros was nibbling a chocolate biscuit. That, and an apple, was her lunch. They were exceptionally busy on the ward and had admitted two emergencies earlier plus one planned admission. Jessie was doing a split duty and went at one, so Ros missed lunch. She didn't mind, and was happier staying on the ward.

It was unfortunate that it should be Max Barrington who caught her. She wasn't supposed to lunch in the office, but if the hierarchy didn't send anyone to relieve her, they must just accept it.

Her mouth was full, when she became aware of the surgeon—a weary-looking surgeon, lines of fatigue etched deeply into his dark face. Lines of anger, too.

Fury might be a more appropriate word for his feelings, Ros decided, hastily chewing and swallowing the offending biscuit. She jumped to her feet, face flushed, ready for the reprimand she was sure to get.

'Why are you always in the office when I come?' he enquired, his voice gentle. Too gentle, the calm before the storm.

'I'm not, sir. Quite often I'm tending to patients and you don't see me at all,' she said firmly, meeting his hooded gaze.

'I see. I thought you did not care to be with the

patients, Staff Nurse. It occurred to me that you preferred office-work.'

Sarcasm wouldn't get him anywhere, Ros was determined on that. 'No, sir,' she said politely, and waited.

'I will not have impudence!' he thundered, and Ros nearly shot out of her skin.

'I wasn't! Being impudent, I mean,' she said, her voice rising in indignation.

'Then get on with your work! Do you not realise there is a ward full of very sick people out there!' he said, his voice whipping her. 'Yet you sit here, *eating*!'

He made eating sound the greatest of sins and Ros found it hard not to retort. Yet nothing good would come from answering him back. Instead, she said quietly: 'I am at lunch, Mr Barrington. There wasn't time to go to the canteen so I'm having a few minutes' break here. If anyone on the ward needs me they know I'll come.'

'Give me the notes of Miss Andrea Skilton,' he commanded, holding out his hand.

Shaken and distressed, Ros put the case-notes into his hand. She'd been reading them while she had her ten-minute break, not wanting to waste a moment of the ward's time.

He settled down in the chair beside the desk, and Ros went to the cabinet, intent on reading more notes. She wasn't going to rush away, tail down, just because the consultant had raged at her. If he didn't like her manner he could report her to Miss Merry.

Would he? The unhappy thought nagged at her as she settled back in Jessie's chair.

'What do you make of this girl?'

'If you mean Miss Skilton, she doesn't appear too bad at the moment,' Ros said, cautiously. 'I saw her about twenty minutes ago and she'd settled in well. I think she is glad to be here,' she went on, even more cautiously, expecting Max to pounce on her any moment.

'I agree,' he surprised her by saying, though the ill-humour didn't leave his face. 'It is a very trying condition. Sometimes it is made worse by relatives.'

Ros nodded. 'She's mother-ridden. I admitted the girl but it was mother who answered all the questions!'

'I will see her now. Ahmed has seen her, also Everett?'

'Yes, sir. While you were in theatre. Mr Scott must have finished early.'

'He did. I sent him to lunch. It appears he came here instead. He has an appetite for work, that one,' he said, grudgingly.

'Yes, he has sir. He's a very good worker,' Ros agreed, earnestly.

'A good worker or a quick worker, I wonder?' the surgeon finished, enigmatically, then strode from the office leaving Ros to wonder whether she should accompany him. She *was* at lunch, after all. But of course she must. She couldn't think why she hesitated.

He was at the bedside by the time Ros arrived. Andrea was in the side-ward, a four-bedder, the only other occupant being Mrs Sinden, a lady due for discharge.

'I wondered if you were coming, Staff Nurse,' the surgeon murmured, caustically, then he turned the full force of his charm on Andrea Skilton, who was twenty-two and looked sixteen. A tall, fair girl with lovely blue-grey eyes, she blossomed under the surgeon's admiring eye and Ros couldn't help wishing he gazed at her that way.

It was purely professional. He was simply trying to put

the shy young woman at ease, and probably he was unaware of the effect his charm had on women. Ros knew only too well!

'Why is Miss Skilton in this small room?' he enquired of Ros, who explained that the main ward was full and they simply could not squeeze in another bed anywhere.

'But tomorrow we could move two patients in here and Miss Skilton can go to the main ward, but . . .' Ros hesitated, unwilling to go into details as Miss Skilton was drinking in every word. 'I thought Miss Skilton would be better here. It isn't so noisy and the bathroom is nearer,' Ros hurried on, seeing by his frown that he did not approve.

'Find room *today* for Miss Skilton. Near the further end of the ward, certainly, but today if you please.'

'Yes, sir.' Ros swallowed, and kept her voice polite. Oh, how she longed to be a ward sister. Then she could tell him what she thought of doctors who re-arranged her ward to suit themselves!

Andrea lifted her lovely eyes to the surgeon's, then hesitantly put a hand on his arm. Ros gazed down at the hand, slender and white, with long tapering fingers. Such a slim, almost fleshless hand.

Ros' eyes softened. The poor creature was wasting away, becoming skeletal, and she was such a pretty girl. Her own age, too.

His examination completed, Max spoke a few reassuring words to the patient then strode from the room.

Ros was about to follow, promising to return as soon as she could, when Andrea called her back: 'Is he married, Nurse? He's gorgeous!'

'I'm not sure. You'll have to ask him,' Ros called gaily, then escaped. Poor Andrea Skilton if she was falling for that cold-hearted beast!

The surgeon was waiting for Ros outside the office.

'Newly admitted patients do not go straight into side-rooms, Staff Nurse!' he blazed, and Ros quailed.

'I know, but . . .' She tried to explain that Jessie, having assessed Andrea's needs, decided she would be better off in a small room just until the ward quietened down, but Max wouldn't let her explain.

'There can be no excuses, Staff Nurse! I would like you to leave. I have said so before!'

'Have you?' Ros quavered, remembering only too well his words on the night of the party.

'I cannot tolerate you on my ward. Why not go to medical? Or babies, perhaps. I like babies,' he said, unexpectedly.

'I'm glad you do!' Ros said, tartly. 'I hope you have loads of them!'

She knew she'd gone too far, but it was too late now.

A muscle twitched at the corner of his jaw. 'I think we have come to the parting of the ways, Staff Nurse,' he said, sternly, his features once more expressionless, carved from granite.

'Yes, sir, I believe we have,' she retorted, not letting him see how dispirited she was. Let him think she didn't care.

When Jessie returned to the ward Ros passed on the surgeon's instructions but didn't mention the blazing row. She guessed Jessie would get to hear of it sooner or later.

Because the ward was humming with activity, Ros elected to stay on after four-thirty when her duty should have finished. She stayed until suppertime and consequently was still on the ward when Max Barrington telephoned Jessie and asked her to replace her junior staff nurse.

'Oh, Ros! Why can't you get on with the man?' Jessie asked in despair as she and a dejected Ros faced each other in the sluice, where Ros had been emptying a bedpan.

'I don't know. But you said yourself no-one gets on well with him!' Ros cried, defensively.

'Not *well*, no, but they make the effort. You and he, you seem to strike sparks off each other. There's some chemistry there, but you repel each other, instead of attracting.'

'I know, I know. Is he going to complain to Miss Merry?' He would take pleasure in that, Ros decided, unfairly.

But she was wrong. 'No, he said it wasn't a formal complaint. It was just that he didn't feel happy with you being in charge sometimes. Anything could go wrong, he said, then where would she turn?' Jessie went on, half-joking: 'He sounded as if he was more concerned for you than he was for the ward!'

'Rubbish!' Ros snapped. As if he cared a fig for her!

Nonetheless, if a consultant wanted rid of a nurse, there were ways and means. Ros turned the problem over and over as she lay in her bed. The street-light cast a faint glow into her room and she stared at it for a while. Although tired she could not sleep. Too much had happened on the ward for her brain to rest.

Then there was the fight with Max Barrington. If only he realised she loved him! But life was full of 'if onlys' and he would never know. If he wanted her to move then she ought to go. He could make life very unpleasant for her otherwise. Non-co-operation it was called. Her working days would become so miserable she would be glad to leave the hospital, never mind the ward. Where to go was the problem. She loved surgical nursing, intended to make it her specialty. Medical wards weren't the same—there it was one long slog. Bedpans, back-trolleys, and so on. An unending grind. And there wasn't so much variety in the type of illness seen. Max had mentioned babies but Ros hadn't taken the CMB. The children's ward appealed, though.

Eventually she slept when it was time to waken, and had to hurry, sparsely washed and unbreakfasted, up to Jevington.

Her request for a move had to go through channels and it was nearly the end of the week before it reached the PNO. Ros still hadn't decided where she wanted to go and hit upon the idea of offering to work wherever she was needed most. That would be geriatrics, she thought, but at least she would be well out of harm's way there. And she would be so exhausted at the end of the day that she would sleep like a log, instead of lying awake tormenting herself with thoughts of Max Barrington!

She took only one day off that week but didn't visit Fairhaven. Her memories were too tender for that. He would spend the coming weekend there, she guessed, with Danielle and Anne-Marie. Were they officially engaged now? she wondered. By now the large solitaire must be on the third finger of Danielle's left hand, sparkling with white fire.

That was all Danielle was interested in—Max's money, a share of Fairhaven, and the prestige that went with being the wife of a consultant, whereas Ros cared only for the man himself. They could be as poor as poor, but with him she would be content, would ask for nothing more than to be his wife and Anne-Marie's mother. Mother to his sons, as well! Max ought to have sons.

The interview with the PNO was for Friday afternoon

but just before Friday lunches were served, an episode on the ward put thoughts of the interview right out of Ros' head.

The morning began as any other, with reports, medicines, breakfast. Night Staff Nurse had reported that Andrea Skilton was restless, and woke several times during the night complaining of fatigue, sleeplessness, pins and needles. Each time the malady had been in a different part of her body and Night Nurse concluded that it was more mental than physical, perhaps a reaction to being among strange people. Ward noises at night caused a problem, too. Although everything possible was done to keep noise to a minimum, the corridors *were* noisy and, together with essential lighting, caused sleepless nights for many, or would have without sedation.

Ros had made a special point of getting to know Andrea. They were of similar age, and both enjoyed the quieter pleasures of life—a book, a country walk, tea with friends. Andrea had no steady boy-friend. Ros hoped they might become friends once Andrea was discharged. They had one other thing in common—they both fancied Max Barrington!

Andrea would like Fairhaven, it would be restful for her, but Ros didn't like to presume on their friendship. She must wait and see how Andrea felt once the op, if any, was over. The colitis was often treated medically, and an operation on so young a person would not be undertaken lightly. Max was, Ros knew, hoping the condition would undergo a remission so that the operation could be put off. She might well be returned to medical, after a brief rest, or even discharged. But first she must be built up. And Andrea responded well to the rest. Yet there was something troubling her and try as she might, Ros couldn't completely gain her confidence.

Now, as the first trays were being unloaded from the trolley, SEN Brown ran up to tell Jessie that Andrea was missing from the dayroom.

'She was sitting there, good as gold, Staff!' Madge Brown assured them. 'Playing Scrabble we were, though she couldn't get anything right. She wasn't concentrating, seemed preoccupied.'

Ros and Jessie exchanged worried glances. Then Jessie organised a search, sending the others off in various directions while she continued to serve the lunches. Work must go on. She would set a full-scale search in motion if Andrea wasn't on the ward or the periphery.

As luck would have it, Ros found her before that became necessary. Andrea was sitting on the balcony of the ward next door and the Sister had been about to phone Jevington about her. She was perilously close to the edge and should not have been there.

No patient was allowed on that balcony because of the risk of a fatal fall. When more money was available, it was to be turned into a dayroom similar to the one on Jevington. Until then the glass door leading out to it was kept locked. Yet somehow Andrea had found a way through.

It was certainly locked now and Ros tapped gently on the glass to attract Andrea's attention. Andrea, turning from her contemplation of the blue sky above, shook her head.

'Please, Andrea. We're very short on the ward. I can't stay long!' Ros pleaded, and Andrea reluctantly unlocked the door, standing well clear so that Ros couldn't grab hold of her, which had been her original intention.

'Whatever are you doing out here?' Ros scolded, hurrying to the edge and looking down. It wasn't a long drop but quite sufficient to break a leg. Not having any great head for heights she was glad to move away.

Andrea stood, eyeing her sulkily. 'It's no use your telling me to come in because I won't,' she said, firmly, and Ros affected surprise.

'You ought to come in—you'll miss lunch otherwise, but . . .' she shrugged as if it didn't matter in the slightest, and Andrea looked put out.

Play it by ear, Ros, she told herself, believing that a show of disinterest would be the best way. 'It's cold out here. Do you enjoy fresh air *that* much?'

'No, but the ward's full of stuffy old women. They don't understand!' Andrea burst out, beginning to march to and fro across the spacious balcony.

Behind the patient's moving figure Ros could see nurses gathering, a porter—and Max Barrington! Deliberately ignoring them, she continued talking to her patient, trying to make her see that the other patients couldn't possibly understand her condition if theirs were so much different.

'Some of them have daughters of your age, though. I expect one or two would like to mother you!'

Andrea's face darkened. 'I get enough mothering, thank you!'

Ros shrugged, hands in dress pockets. While Andrea's back was turned. Ros waved away the onlookers and, thankfully, they took the hint. She saw Max ushering them away. If Andrea thought they might make a rush for her she would back away, and might easily fall over the balcony. It wasn't worth the risk.

It was chilly on the balcony. The sun went behind a dark grey cloud and Ros eyed it, anxiously. 'I'm going in. There's a downpour coming any minute. Hurry up, we'll get wet!' Catching the other girl by surprise, Ros urged her towards the glass-door, hoping that help

wasn't too far away, as Andrea began to struggle. Lucki-
ly, a nurse and the porter were waiting and all three
helped an unwilling Andrea back into the ward.

'There! We'll be warm now and I expect you are
hungry!' Ros chatted away as they escorted Andrea
down the ward and out into the corridor. There was no
sign of the consultant and Ros supposed he'd been called
away. But he had not. He was standing by Jevington
ward office as they approached and he beckoned Andrea
forward. Ros made as if to follow but was waved away.

Cold, annoyed, and hurt by the surgeon's peremptory
dismissal of her, Ros went to help with the lunches and
to give Jessie a report on the incident. Ros was convinced that if any blame was to attach to the staff
somehow Max Barrington would pin it on her!

Ros's interview with Miss Merry was cordial. The first
thing the PNO did was to congratulate Ros on her
cool-headedness and presence of mind when persuading
Andrea Skilton to return to Jevington.

'She could easily have fallen, Staff Nurse. You may
have saved her life,' Miss Merry assured Ros, brown
eyes smiling approvingly at her.

Embarrassed, Ros tried to make light of it, then Miss
Merry abruptly changed the subject: 'Why do you want
to leave Jevington? You get on well with Staff Nurse
Bradley, don't you?'

Ros hastened to say that it had nothing to do with
Jessica Bradley. 'She's my friend, Miss Merry. But I feel
I need a change . . .' her voice trailed off at the disbeliev-
ing expression on the PNO's face.

'You haven't been there long enough to need a
change,' Miss Merry pointed out. There was a long
pause while Ros tried to think of something concrete to

say, then Miss Merry went on: 'It isn't Mr Barrington, by any chance?'

Ros nodded without speaking. What could she say, anyway?

'It may be for the best. I feel he needs a more mature staff nurse, an older woman,' Miss Merry said, and Ros silently agreed with her. It was agreed that Ros would stay a further week, then be on relief until a suitable post could be found for her.

A dispirited Ros made her way back to Jevington. After the week was up she might never see the surgeon again, and perhaps it would be for the best.

It was the Annual Hospital Fete and Open Day at the end of her last week. It always attracted big crowds, people coming in from as far afield as Cambridge and Ipswich.

Ros had offered to help run a stall and was landed with the white elephant stall, assisting the Administrator's wife. Because she'd had only one day off the previous week she had three days off before starting her relief duties so would be free all weekend and Monday, too.

She so longed to get away from St Ann's, to spend the weekend in her own home, but Max would be there and all this did nothing to sweeten her feelings towards him. As far as she was concerned if she never saw him again, it would be too soon!

At the end of the day there was the usual Hospital Ball, a grand affair where everyone dressed up in their most formal attire. Consultants mixed with student nurses, administrators with junior doctors, and a good time was had by all. Ros had been to only one previous ball, with Jessie and Brian, and although she enjoyed the music, only one person apart from Brian had asked her

to dance and that was Albert, the hall porter, who tried
to dance with everyone. True, Mr Turner, the consultant whose place Max had taken, did sit out one dance
with her. He couldn't dance because he'd fractured his
ankle.

It wasn't the same as having a partner, though, and
Ros felt a definite wallflower. This year, despite Jessie's
pleading, she decided she certainly wasn't going. She
would be just as happy in her room or downstairs in the
Nurses' sitting-room, watching the colour TV.

The day before, as Ros was supervising a student
nurse removing sutures, a head poked around the curtain. It was a head with a thatch of fair hair, not black,
and Ros smiled warmly at Everett.

He waited patiently until the task was completed, then
beckoned Ros over. 'The ball. Am I too late, Cinders?
Are you fixed up?'

'Fixed up?' Ros' eyes widened in disbelief. Surely the
popular Everett Scott wasn't asking *her* to go as his
partner? But he was.

'Thought I wouldn't make it, but old Max the Magnificent offered to do my round. Walking the wards will do
him good, he said!'

'Mr Barrington?' Ros queried, her voice faint.

Everett nodded, emphatically. 'The very same. Said
he couldn't go to the ball.'

'Oh?' Couldn't Danielle get there? She might be in
France for all Ros knew. If so, perhaps Max wasn't
spending his weekend at Fairhaven. She must find out. If
he wasn't, she could at least spend Sunday there. A
relaxing day at home would put her in the right mood for
whatever tasks she had to perform next Tuesday.

'Say you'll come, sweet Rosamunde!' Everett begged,
laughing at her, and she nodded.

'Mm. Yes, please. I wasn't going—not without a partner, but . . .'

'What about old what's-his-name? The legal eagle. The one you spent a naughty night with?'

Ros blushed, and Everett laughed all the more, but she couldn't be angry with him. 'I did *not* spend a naughty night with him. As a matter of fact it never occurred to me to invite him,' she went on, wonderingly. It was true. She was bemoaning the fact that she couldn't go to the ball without a partner but it hadn't occurred to her that Barry would be willing to escort her. He would, she had no doubt, but she didn't want him!

She wondered why she hadn't realised it before. She liked the man but didn't spare him a thought once he was out of her sight. Poor, poor Barry, who cared for her. But it was for the best. As she felt nothing for him, she ought not to encourage him.

'I'll pick you up at seven-thirty then,' Everett was saying. 'You won't be staying at your mansion, will you?'

'No!' Ros was in no doubt about that. 'I'll wait for you in the doorway of the Annexe. And thank you, Everett.'

'For what? I'm escorting a pretty young nurse to the ball for my own wicked ends! I don't expect thanks as well!'

Ros laughed, and the happy smile still lingered on her face as she met the black, disapproving eyes of Max Barrington. Everett had gone and Max was about to enter Jessie's office. There was a stony silence, while Ros racked her brain for something to say. Anything. 'I'll say goodbye then, Mr Barrington,' she said, chin held high. 'This is my last day on Jevington,' she went on, as he remained silent, aloof.

'I know,' he replied, indifference in his voice. 'I

think leaving was a wise decision, Staff Nurse. Good-night.'

With that, he marched into the office, closing the door in her face. She stepped back as if she'd been struck. If she had wanted any evidence of his feelings towards her there it was. Leaving was a wise decision. *He* thought so too. He was pleased she was going!

With eyes smarting, Ros went back to the ward. If she'd thought he might praise her for saving Andrea Skilton, who had now gone back to a medical ward where Ros visited her, she was mistaken. If she believed he might have said how sorry he was to see her go, or how he hoped she would enjoy her new post, well, she was mistaken about that, too. He simply did not care, and that hurt most of all.

Ros was ready by seven o'clock the following evening. The fete went well and the white elephant stall had done a brisk trade, to her surprise.

She wore the black dress, because it was the only suitable dress she possessed and because it brought back memories of the house-warming. Memories of Max taking her in his arms in the moonlit garden.

Vexed because she hadn't intended thinking about the surgeon, Ros snuggled closer into her pretty white lacy jacket. Everett had a car of sorts so she wouldn't get too cold. She was gazing down at her elegant black high-heeled sandals and wondering how much dancing she could do in them when the phone rang. There was no-one around so Ros answered it, hoping she wouldn't have to traipse all over the Home searching for a particular nurse. The call could be for anyone.

But it was for her. Everett's voice was angry and for a moment Ros couldn't take in what he was saying.

'You *can't* take me to the ball, did you say? And what was that about Mr Barrington?'

The line crackled, partly with Everett's anger, she thought. 'I said he's gone back on his word. Says he is going to the ball after all and would I mind staying on duty!' Everett swore, and Ros held the receiver away from her ear in amazement.

'Everett! That wasn't a nice word! But surely he can't do that?' Ros was almost in tears. Max Barrington had no right!

'He can and he has,' Everett said, doggedly. 'But he says I can see the end of the ball, that he will relieve me. I believe his girl-friend has returned and he wants to give her a couple of dances.'

Danielle again. That Everett and his date might be eagerly looking forward to going obviously cut no ice with Max the Magnificent. Oh, no! What *he* wanted was paramount.

'Will you wait for me, pet? Though I shall be so tired by ten that I won't be much of a partner,' Everett went on, dejectedly, and Ros' anger burned afresh.

Willingly she said she would wait, then rang off. Poor Everett. That monster! For two pins she would . . .

'Ah! Quite ready, are you?' a familiar voice enquired as Max Barrington strode into the hallway of the Annexe.

When a dismayed Ros didn't reply, he took her by the arm. Before she knew where she was she was in his Jaguar, being settled in the front seat, with a tartan rug being gently tucked around her knees. Although his touch was cool, impersonal, his nearness set Ros' teeth on edge and she held herself rigidly in case he noticed her agitation.

Only when he set the powerful car in motion did Ros

come to realise that she'd virtually been kidnapped!

'Mr Barrington,' she began, icily, 'may I know where you are taking me?'

'To the ball, naturally. Where else would I take the beautiful princess?' he mocked, and her hand itched to slap him.

'Everett Scott is taking me to the ball—later on. I was going back to my room to wait for him,' Ros added.

'Oh, he comes to your room, does he?' For some reason Max was annoyed, and Ros gloated.

'Why not? That part of the Nurses' Home is for trained nurses. We don't have any old-fashioned rules about no male visitors in rooms! This is the permissive age, sir,' she said, tongue in cheek, knowing how he hated her to call him 'sir' off-duty.

He didn't rise to the bait. 'I must remember that English girls are permissive, Staff Nurse,' he said, huskily. And could there have been a hint of laughter in his tone?

Ros didn't say any more, and when they reached the Village Hall where the event was always held, she was reluctant to leave the luxurious car. Why did he bring her? Did he expect her to sit in a corner of the hall and wait for Everett, while he danced away with Danielle?

'I haven't a partner, Mr Barrington, so if you intend to dump me in a corner I would rather wait here for Everett.' Seeing he did not understand she went on: 'Here. In the car. I don't want to sit alone.'

'Foolish fanciful child,' he said, softly, those deep, liquid eyes fixed on her face, devouring her.

'What did you say?' she asked, wonderingly.

He repeated it. 'You remember? That day at Fairhaven. You told me you used to be called that. You still are in many ways.' He brushed back a strand of honey hair that had strayed, and she trembled at his touch. She couldn't help it.

She wore her hair up in what she considered a mature style and he frowned. 'Such hair! Like silk. It should be free so that all may admire it.'

Breathlessly she waited for him to unpin it but his hand dropped away and he muttered something in what she supposed was Hungarian.

Disappointed but determined not to show it, Ros got out and pretended an interest in the village hall that she did not feel. Lights blazed everywhere although it wasn't yet dark. The car-park was full, and a few people she knew called a greeting to her, as they passed. One of them, a ward sister, did a quick double-take on seeing Ros' partner.

By tomorrow it would be all over the hospital, Ros thought. Little Nurse Hayward being dated by the magnificent Max Barrington! She wouldn't have a minute's peace. Never mind, they would learn better once he began dancing with Danielle.

She almost asked where Danielle was but bit the words back just in time. She would know soon enough.

When she hesitantly made her way to the main part of the Hall after leaving her wrap, Max surprised her by swinging her into a dance straightaway. It was an energetic number and didn't require the partners to hold each other. Didn't require a dancer to actually *have* a partner so Ros supposed Danielle Dubois wouldn't mind.

While they danced Ros glanced around but could not see the glamorous Frenchwoman. She saw many faces she knew though. There was Miss Merry, Mr Turner, and a great many nurses she knew by sight. Jessie couldn't get away till later and Ros missed her friend. If ever she needed a friend now was the time!

Afterwards Max guided her to a table which he'd reserved and they sat out the next dance in a companionable silence, drinks to hand. He had a large whisky while Ros nervously sipped a Martini, aware that she must make the one drink last all evening. She would need something to hide behind once Danielle arrived.

Doctors stopped to speak to Max as they passed, and Ros sat, unnoticed, a sad smile pinned to her mouth. She would not let anyone see how sad, how alone, she felt. And where was Danielle? Once more her lovely eyes searched for the blonde Danielle, but the place was so crowded it was difficult to see.

'Are you seeking anyone I know?' Max asked, quietly, and Ros disconcerted, shrugged.

'There are lots of people I know,' she said, as he apparently expected an answer.

'Ah, yes, but not the attractive Everett Scott. He is busy, I think,' Max went on, smugly.

'You *think*!' Ros spluttered. 'You know quite well he's busy!'

'Rank has its privileges!' he said lightly, with a smug smile.

Ros was about to snap at him but something in his eyes stopped her. The smile didn't reach them. The dark depths were as cold and as enigmatic as ever, and Ros shivered. He frightened and disturbed her when he gave her that cold-eyed look, like being plunged into an icy river, and she took another sip of her drink.

Then a soft, slow number started and Ros found herself once more in the surgeon's arms, this time being held closely. Rather *too* closely, she felt, but wasn't complaining!

She could feel the heat of his body, smell his spicy after-shave and closed her eyes in bliss. This couldn't last but she intended to make the most of every second.

How smart Max was in his dinner jacket, narrow-fitting dark trousers, plain white shirt. If she opened her eyes just a crack she could see the unusual gold cufflinks he wore. They were set with a tiny diamond, yet on him they did not look effeminate. She wished she had some jewellery to wear. Aunt Gwen had one or two good pieces which Ros had inherited, but they were kept in the bank, Ros having nowhere in the Nurses' Home to keep them. She made do with just earrings—golden horseshoes which were not expensive.

The next dance was an old-fashioned waltz, and he held her closer if that was possible, and Ros' cup of happiness was full. By now she'd convinced herself that he had made Everett stay at St Ann's because he himself wanted to take her to the ball. He cared! No, she thought wryly, he didn't care in the way she did but he must like her, surely? She was almost sure now that for some reason he had not invited Danielle to the occasion. Perhaps she would have been bored, or it could be that she was baby-sitting.

The thought that Danielle was staying at home looking after Anne-Marie while Ros danced with the woman's fiancé pleased her, and she was about to mention Danielle when she felt Max stiffen and move away from her.

Again he made a curt comment in Hungarian, and Ros turned puzzled eyes up to his face. But he wasn't looking at her and she spun round to find Danielle Dubois almost upon them.

'Max, my dear! I am sorry to be late!' Danielle cooed, ignoring Ros completely.

She felt Max's arms drop away, and with a muttered apology he escorted both girls to his table.

Ros went white, more with shock and hurt than anger. How could he do this to her? How could he! Because he knew Danielle would be late, he decided to amuse himself with Ros, uncaring that he'd deprived her of her partner. He was simply using her, making a convenience of Ros because her feelings didn't matter a scrap to him!

The two girls sat down at the table while Max went in search of another chair and more drinks. Ros could feel Danielle's cold blue eyes on her but she stared at the door rather than meet the Frenchwoman's gaze.

When Max returned with the drinks she would make polite excuses then escape, walk all the way back if necessary. Max Barrington had humiliated her enough for one evening.

CHAPTER ELEVEN

A SUBDUED Ros was preparing her lunch at Fairhaven the following day when she heard the squeal of tyres outside.

Alarmed, she poked her head out of the kitchen window convinced there had been an accident. But there was only one car and it belonged to Max Barrington, an angry-looking Max, who stormed into the kitchen before Ros had a chance to even think, let alone act.

'Where is she? What have you done with her?' he snapped, his fingers fastening cruelly about her slender wrists.

'Who? W . . . what do you mean?' Ros was first startled then angry. 'Let me go! Save your charming touch for that . . . that woman!'

'Which woman?' he asked, face dark with anger, but he released her and she rubbed her arm ruefully.

'Miss Dubois! The woman you knew would be late so you amused yourself with a poor little staff nurse while you waited!' Her voice rose, then she broke off with a sob. There was no point in arguing, no point in telling him a few home truths, the man had a hide like a rhino.

'Leave Danielle out of this,' he said, coldly. 'Where is Anne-Marie? I have come to take her home.'

'Anne-Marie?' Ros echoed. 'She isn't here as far as I know. I cleaned the house from top to bottom this morning so I should know. Has . . . has something happened to her?'

'Little girls have been known to disappear and not be

174

seen alive again,' Max said, more gently, seeing her white face.

'B . . . but when did you see her last?' Ros, aghast, sank down onto the kitchen chair, glad of its support. Glad too, of Max's arms which he put around her.

'Earlier this morning. She had her milk drink in the kitchen then I went to my bedroom to work on some papers,' Max explained. 'I have a working housekeeper. She lives in the village but takes care of Anne-Marie when I am out. She was looking after Anne-Marie last night, when I was at the ball.'

'I thought Danielle did that?' Ros said, half to herself.

'Danielle, yes. She said you told Anne-Marie she could come and stay any time she liked. That was a foolish offer to make to a child. If you did,' he added, thoughtfully. He was behind the chair and bent over to see her face.

Ros gazed up at him, unflinchingly. 'No, I didn't.'

He sighed, a brief smile touching his mouth. 'I thought not, but I had to be sure. Danielle said . . .' he hesitated and Ros waited, wondering what else the vicious woman had told him.

'She said you might have lured Anne-Marie here, to pay me back for deserting you last night.'

'Pay you back!' Ros screamed, jumping up, her long hair in a cloud about her. 'If she thinks that it shows what sort of woman she is!'

He shrugged. 'It is of no consequence. We must find Anne-Marie.'

'Yes, of course.' He and Danielle must both be worried, no matter what catty remarks the woman had made about Ros. Anne-Marie was going to become Danielle's step-daughter.

'I will search the outbuildings if you go over the house

again. Look in all the cupboards,' Max ordered, and Ros scurried off.

There was no Anne-Marie anywhere in the cottage. That much was certain. After searching all the likely places Ros looked in all the unlikely ones, but no child. There was the pool. She could have fallen in . . .

Max was there when Ros came to a panting stop at the poolside, and he shook his head. 'She isn't in a shed. We must search the garden but . . .' He left the sentence unfinished, and Ros put a consoling hand on his arm. He patted her hand absently, then they separated. They met up again after a futile search.

'It . . . it isn't likely she was here, Max,' Ros said, unconsciously using his Christian name. 'She could hardly have walked and there is only one bus today. That went straight past, I saw it.'

'I will notify the police now. Pity Fairhaven isn't on the telephone,' Max began, when a taxi drew up and out stepped a grey-haired woman, with a weary, scruffy Anne-Marie in tow.

'Anne-Marie!' The little girl ran into her father's arms then squirmed out of them again.

'I won't go! I simply won't go!' she stormed, then ran to Ros and buried her face in Ros' paisley skirt. 'Don't let them send me!'

With some difficulty, Ros soothed the child, remembering that diverting a child's attention away from its grievance was always a good ploy. She hurried her into the kitchen and produced a rather liquid ice she'd intended to eat after her lunch. She'd taken it out of the icebox too early.

Anne-Marie took the bowl of ice-cream, then, clean girl that she was, asked if she could wash her hands. 'And my hair! It's full of spiders webs!' she moaned, sounding so like a little adult that Ros had to suppress a smile.

Max and the grey-haired woman followed them in and Max introduced her as Mrs Bardwell, his housekeeper.

'Anne-Marie was at home, in the cottage, all the time,' Max said crossly. 'Hiding in the coal-shed, of all places!'

'She looks as if she was! She's upstairs, washing, now!' Ros grinned.

'That shed is generally kept locked but the lock broke. Yet we looked in there—at least Miss Dubois did. How she missed her is the wonder!' Mrs Bardwell put in.

'W . . . where is Miss Dubois?' Ros asked. 'Is she still out hunting for her future daughter. I mean . . . she'll be worried,' she faltered at the expression of distaste on Max's dark face. 'I'm sorry,' she finished, miserably. She ought not to have mentioned it in front of the housekeeper.

'Miss Dubois is not out looking for Anne-Marie!' Mrs Bardwell broke in. 'She's gone back to her own place. In a proper fuss she was. Said as how the master wasn't going to send that brat away to school so she wasn't going to wed him!' Mrs Bardwell went on, clearly pleased. 'Said as how he'd have to get down on his knees and beg her!' She delivered this last remark accompanied by a triumphant smile. 'So I tells her—get back to Paris then, my fine lady. The master isn't a man to get down on his knees for *any* woman!'

Max's husky chuckle broke the astonished silence. Ros joined in but knew Danielle wouldn't take the hint. She would not pass up the chance of becoming Mrs Max Barrington. Ros couldn't blame her, either.

Max had paid off the taxi so he arranged to take Mrs Bardwell back to her own home while Anne-Marie demolished the ice-cream in Ros' kitchen. She wasn't as hungry as might be expected since she'd taken a large helping of sandwiches into the coal-shed with her!

While Max was away the whole story came pouring out. Anne-Marie had overheard Danielle telling her father that Anne-Marie must go away to school once they were married. Danielle could not, it seemed, bear the child around all the time. When Anne-Marie was dressed up for a special occasion and put on her party manners with her party dress, that was fine. But when she behaved like a normal little girl, that didn't suit Danielle.

Reading between the lines Ros gathered that Anne-Marie took up too much of Papa's time—time Danielle felt should be spent with her. She did not, it seemed, live with Max at his cottage. She had a flat in Ipswich. That pleased Ros more than anything! To know that the man she loved hadn't been sharing his home with Danielle. Perhaps Danielle hadn't slept at Fairhaven, either.

They were firm friends by the time the bronze Jaguar returned. Anne-Marie was full of plans to have goldfish in the big pond just beyond the orchard, but Ros told her they must wait and see what Papa said.

Papa smiled indulgently when he heard about the goldfish but, as he pointed out, who would tend the fish?

Anne-Marie's face fell and Ros longed to comfort her. Memories of her own childhood came flooding back, of having no-one to comfort her, but Max was right on this occasion. There would be no-one to see that the fish were all right.

'There is the new gardener, of course, but I cannot ask him,' Max said firmly, and Ros cuddled the child to her.

There *was* a solution to the problem, and Ros wondered if she had the courage to take the final step. To give up Fairhaven, offer her share to the surgeon. Then he and Anne-Marie and, she supposed, Danielle, would live here as a family, and Anne-Marie could have her goldfish. Perhaps a puppy, as well.

She brightened. Whatever the sacrifice cost her it would be worth it. Anne-Marie would be happy and so, too, would Max, the man she adored—when she wasn't hating him!

'Will you both stay to lunch? I'm expecting a guest but there's plenty . . .' Ros broke off at the stiffness of the surgeon's expression.

'A guest? Whom are you expecting?'

'Why, Everett. Everett Scott. When he came off-duty last night he was too tired to take me back to the ball so I thought I'd give him a meal today. The poor dear,' she added, just to annoy Max.

'I am normally here at weekends, Rosalyn,' he said, tightly. 'I do not intend to spend what remains of my weekend with my registrar! After all the trauma I shall expect a quiet afternoon. Please see that your . . . guest does not disturb me.'

Max walked quickly towards the study, leaving Ros alone with Anne-Marie. The child gazed up with puzzled eyes, and quickly Ros found her a few simple chores to keep her occupied. She must tell Max of her decision before it was too late.

He glared when Ros nervously entered the study. 'I . . . would you like my half of Fairhaven?' she burst out, her rehearsed speech going out of her head.

'You wish to sell me the other half of Fairhaven?' he said, slowly, coming towards her.

Ros backed away until she felt the door behind her,

cutting off her retreat. 'Yes. You ought to have the whole of Fairhaven. Then . . . then Anne-Marie could have her goldfish and a puppy.'

'A dog now? What else?' he sounded amused as he stopped only inches from her.

Her mind went blank for a moment. The after-shave wafted across to her. It was a sophisticated scent but he looked anything but sophisticated this morning, in faded jeans and a black shirt. She lowered her gaze and could just see the big buckle on the narrow belt at his waist, as she went on, hurriedly: 'When you get married you will want the whole of Fairhaven. It isn't fair that you would have to share it. You must have a whole house.'

'Indeed? And what will you do, my foolish fanciful child?' Gently, he tilted her head back, forcing her to meet his enigmatic gaze.

'I have other plans,' she lied, then watched, fascinated, as his brows drew together in a frown.

'Plans? What plans? Do they include my registrar?' he barked.

'They might.' With an effort she kept her eyes on his, the violet in them becoming marked as she fought down the pain. 'It isn't any of your business, sir,' she added, for good measure.

His face hardened, the resemblance to a granite-hewn Greek god becoming more pronounced.

'Then you intend marrying him.' It was a statement more than a question. 'Where will you live?'

Ros shrugged, nonchalantly, and Max turned away. 'As you say,' he went on, his back to her, 'when I marry I shall want a home where I can bring my bride. A *complete* house, as you point out. I will buy Fairhaven from you.'

'Th . . . thank you,' she murmured brokenly. Despite

the turmoil over Anne-Marie he hadn't denied he was still marrying Danielle. Poor Anne-Marie. Her life would be a hard one, particularly if her Papa was so besotted with Danielle that he was willing to send his daughter to a boarding-school. Why, she was far too young to be a boarder!

Ros' heart ached for Anne-Marie and for herself, but that was life. There was nothing more she could do, for herself or for the child.

Lunch, when Everett eventually arrived half an hour late, was a strained affair. He and Max kept up a desultory conversation about medical matters, while Anne-Marie concentrated on her food, and Ros sat lost in thought. This, she had already decided, was to be her last day at Fairhaven. As she had to move she intended to make a clean break. She would sleep here tonight, then first thing tomorrow she would walk down the lane to order a taxi back to St Ann's. There was little of hers here, only a few clothes, her transistor. Everything else came with Fairhaven, even the china and bed-linen. All had belonged to Aunt Gwen.

She would keep a small memento of Aunt Gwen, just to remind her of old times, and she was puzzling over what to take when Everett got to his feet, scraping back his chair, noisily.

'Well, I'll be getting back to St Ann's then,' he said, curtly, and Ros stared.

'Aren't you stopping for coffee? And you said you felt like a swim,' her voice trailed off at the angry, tight expression on the face of both men. They must have been arguing and she'd been so wrapped up in her thoughts she hadn't taken any notice!

She saw Everett off, half relieved he had decided to go. With him and Max Barrington glaring at each other all afternoon, it wouldn't have been much fun for anyone!

She put her hand on his sleeve and gazed up at him. 'Please, Everett. Tell me what's wrong. I didn't know Mr Barrington would be here this afternoon, honestly.'

'After the way you said he treated you last night, I'm surprised you even spoke to the man!' Everett said, irritably. 'You told me he and Danielle danced off and left you sitting—that if Jessie and Brian hadn't arrived then you would have sat alone for the rest of the evening!'

Ros, ashamed, nodded. She did tell Everett that, and it was true but exaggerated. If Jessie hadn't arrived she supposed Max would have spared her another dance, but certainly he had no right to think he could escort *two* women to the ball! Even Prince Charming made do with one!

Ros stayed outside after Everett drove away, her suppressed anger at the surgeon boiling up again, coming to the surface. He *had* treated her badly. He had no right to upset poor Everett, either, and she had a good mind to tell him so.

'With whom are you arguing?' a cold voice asked, and Ros, temper still raging, glared at Max.

'I was having a silent argument with you, if you must know!' she snapped. 'You had no business upsetting Everett! He hasn't done you any harm!'

'I put him wise about a few matters. I told him if he married you it didn't mean he was getting Fairhaven as well. I also told him he must look after you, cherish you,' Max went on calmly, and Ros stared. 'He was surprised,' Max added.

Surprised wouldn't be the word for it, Ros mused. Everett must have been astounded!

'He did not seem to know that you and he were engaged so I apologised for the misunderstanding. Just what *did* you mean when you told me you had other plans for your future?' he asked, menacingly.

'It isn't your business. You're marrying Danielle,' Ros said brokenly, not caring now. 'You . . . you only took me to the ball to pass the time away,' she sniffed, unable to forget the mortifying incident.

'But, no!' he denied. 'I did not expect her. I wanted to dance only with you, my little one. I did not invite Danielle.' He swung her round to face him. 'Am I marrying her, Rosalyn? You misunderstood, just as I did.'

'Then who *are* you marrying? Oh, I suppose you were planning for the future, some day when you *do* want to remarry.'

'The future?'

'Yes, when you said you would want a complete house for you and your . . . your bride.'

'Ah, yes, I *did* say that.' He pulled her against him, his eyes hooded. 'If you are not marrying the charming Everett Scott perhaps you would marry me instead?'

'I beg your pardon?' Ros said carefully, not wanting to make an embarrassing mistake. He couldn't be proposing!

But he was. He repeated his words. 'I am difficult to live with, often impossible. I have a terrible temper and I insist on having my own way all the time!' he added, and Ros beamed.

'Yes, *sir*!' She sketched him a salute then snuggled up against him, her eyes closed. It was incredible, too good to be true. Of course he didn't say he loved her, but she mustn't expect too much of him. He obviously wanted her so that would have to do. She would make a home for him and Anne-Marie, his daughter, her daughter, *their* daughter now.

And one day there would be others. A few brothers for Anne-Marie to organise!

His delicate surgeon's fingers began to caress her, sending shivers of delight coursing through her body. He kissed her, tenderly at first, coaxing a response from her, then a car tooted, and they broke apart.

For a second Ros couldn't remember where she was. Only seconds before she knew she'd been in heaven but where was she now?

The bright green sports-car didn't belong to an angel, it belonged to Barry Simpkin, whom she hadn't seen all week. What a time to arrive!

'Ros! I've been at the hospital. Couldn't get any reply from your room!' Barry got out of the car and when Ros would have gone forward to meet him, Max held her back, his fingers locked like a handcuff around her wrist.

'Wait here,' he ordered curtly, and a surprised Ros did as she was told. She might as well get some practice in if he was always going to have his own way!

There was a heated exchange between the two men while Ros made a close study of the swimming pool, trying not to listen. Anne-Marie waved to her from a bedroom window and Ros waved back, glad the child was out of earshot.

The solicitor drove off quickly, his car tearing down the drive, and Ros winced. She'd lost another friend. Was losing her friends and acquaintances too high a price to pay for marriage to the surgeon? She knew it was not. Whatever his faults she loved him, even if he only *wanted* her. Love might come.

There was an awkward silence, then she felt Max's arms around her. 'I apologise. For my hasty temper and for everything else,' he said, huskily. 'If you have changed your mind I will understand.'

'Oh, no!' Aghast, Ros stood on tiptoe, and daringly kissed his cheek. 'No, I haven't changed my mind,' she whispered, her eyes pleading, begging him to understand how she cared.

He ran a finger down the side of her face, and she quivered. 'I will make up to you for your hard childhood. I believe it is what Miss Liston intended. She gave us Fairhaven in the hope we might come to share it permanently.'

'Mm. A legacy of love,' Ros whispered, as he bent to kiss her.

He stopped, mouth poised tantalisingly just above hers. 'Legacy of love? I believe it is. Can it be that you love me a little?' he asked, wonder in his voice. 'But, no! I am impossible, a hard taskmaster. What you call a chauvinist!'

'It is quite possible to love a chauvinist!' Ros laughed, 'I've always loved you,' she went on, shyly, her heart full. She loved him so much, that surely one day he, too, would say he loved her?

Their lips met in a long drawn out kiss, Ros leaning back in his arms, knowing she was safe, protected, cherished.

'Do you truly love me?' he asked again, and she nodded. 'I do. I . . . I know you only want me but . . .' Embarrassed, she broke off, her skin taking on a delicate pink tinge as she thought of all 'wanting' would mean. She would belong to the surgeon, be his completely and utterly.

'Want you?' he whispered, against her mouth. 'Of course I want you. I desire you! Do you hear me!'

'Mm. Yes, master.'

'Less of your cheek, woman!' he growled. 'Also I love you.'

Ros pulled herself out of his embrace. 'Do you? But I thought you just . . . I mean, do you really?' she asked, wonderingly, and he kissed the tip of her pert little nose.

'I always have, though at first you were just a body,' he said gruffly. 'When I was so unkind to you, so keen to get you off my ward, I did it for your sake, my little one. I was no good for you, so old, and with a child.'

'You're not old!' she scolded. 'Anyway, I'll keep you young. So will Anne-Marie.'

'Perhaps there will be others later,' he suggested, nuzzling her ear, and she giggled.

'Do you think Anne-Marie will like me as a mother?' she asked, anxiously.

'We must ask her. But first, one more kiss to keep me going. We will have a big white wedding for you, but we must make plans quickly, eh? I am not a patient man and cannot wait long.'

She opened her mouth as he pressed his lips against hers, then an excited voice broke in:

'Are you in love, then?' Anne-Marie skipped into view, looking up at them with interest. 'I've seen people in love before. They do all soppy things!' she announced.

'Rosalyn is going to be my wife, your new mother,' Max said gently, stroking his daughter's fair head. 'What do you think of that?'

Ros waited anxiously for the child's verdict.

Anne-Marie beamed at them, then put her hand in Ros'. 'Are we a family now then?' she asked, and Ros nodded, too full to speak.

'We really are a family now, Anne-Marie,' Max said,

his eyes on Ros. 'You and me and Rosalyn. Plus the goldfish, eh?'

Ros glanced towards Fairhaven as Max picked up his daughter and hugged her, whilst keeping one arm around Ros' shoulders.

Fairhaven seemed to be smiling, as though pleased that the legacy given in love hadn't been wasted.

Ros knew it would be difficult loving this arrogant, charismatic man, but it would all be worth it. Her heart raced at the thought of belonging to him for the rest of their lives.

They exchanged loving glances, then all three went indoors, to show the cottage they were now a complete family.